SONGS
From The Desert

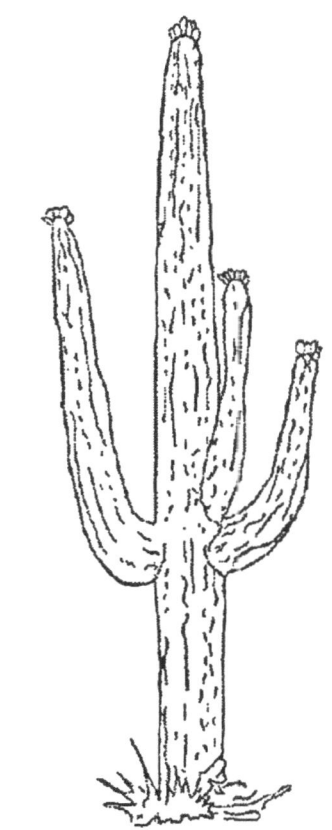

Ann McDermott

Ann McDermott
Desert Drifter Publications
261 Maya Dr.
Litchfield Park, Arizona 85340

E-mail the author at annfmcdermott@gmail.com
Write "Songs From The Desert" in the subject line

Printed in U.S.A.
ISBN: 978-0692247044

In Thanksgiving

I thank the neighbors who helped read and edit, remember and coalesce the stories included in these short essays, written over the course of over ten years time, from the vantage point of a desk at my second story bedroom window overlooking the Sonoran desert I loved calling home. Primary among them were Nel Sosa and Cathy Holler. They not only know which tales are about them, but most of the folks featured in the rest. I am blessed to have had them both as neighbors.

I must also thank the writer's critique group for the input they gave freely. Some were good at coming up with just the right word to improve my own. Some were better at commas and hyphens than I. All helped me improve how I wrote, and gave feedback on how well I was communicating, the great challenge of every author. Over the years, attendance in the group varied, but honorable mention goes to Brendon Marks, Debra Quarles, Anna Marie Burk, Bob Yereance, Bill Whitton, Peggy Kuula, Lea Somes, Laird Sonic, Inez Unruh, Jerry Hayes, Judy Turrentine, Ernie Shaver, and all those others who did not suffer me in silence, but helped refine "the work." It truly is a gift having the free evaluations of other writers. Many are the laughs and encouragements that come of such groups, not to mention the priceless friendships.

Special thanks, too, to Barbara Anderson, who has charge of putting the pieces together to make a whole book. She does the stuff I find most disagreeable. God bless the ones who enjoy doing the tasks for which I have no love.

And lastly, thanks to all those other neighbors who taught me and shared their lives with me, those creatures wild and native to the desert I no longer have just off my back patio. I still do my best to visit once or twice a week with a drive to a bit of remoteness. Town life has some advantages, but one of them is not screech owls, and those kinds of neighbors I miss greatly. For my opportunity to associate with them, I am eternally grateful. That they may speak through me, I offer this.

Contents

Spring

Summer

Spring

Introduction

It starts with a change of awareness, then a change of heart. Nature heals like that: the light and dark of it, the pleasure and pain of it, the beginnings and ends of it.

When my husband died, I was living in Phoenix in a house we'd rented together before he left for Florida to take refresher courses in flying single engine aircraft for the Navy. He'd been flying P-3's, four-engined turboprops, out of Moffett, California. He needed to retrain in the smaller aircraft he was to fly out of Sky Harbor Airport to numerous recruiting centers in Arizona, Colorado and New Mexico, as one of two Navy pilots stationed in Phoenix.

When he and his instructor pilot were both killed, I became a single parent of a 15 month old son, two dogs and a cat. My husband and I had often discussed our mutual dream of living in a rural area. When friends told me of land for sale north of Sun City West, Arizona, acreage with power, water and unpaved roads, I explored it.

Eventually, I bought and built a house in the open, native desert, with the Hieroglyphic Mountains to the north and east, the pine-topped Bradshaws even farther to the north, the White Tank Mountains on the west, and the distant Estrellas on the southern horizon. My nearest neighbors were suddenly saguaro, snakes and scorpion weed.

I appreciated the opportunity to live in desert habitat, yet still have the modern conveniences of dishwashers, microwave ovens and air conditioning. I was enamored of the open horizons and glorious full moons, the sunsets and sun rises. I was not prepared, however, to discover how much this new life played a role in healing me of the grief and pain of early widowhood. The lessons I found awaiting me in my new home, now over twenty years old, shaped a new awareness of life, taught me to love quite differently, embody different values and expectations, and appreciate insecurity and life's fragility. It was a healing I very much needed. It's an awareness that continues unfolding before me as I journey onward.

Now what I love best is writing stories of that desert I find so indispensable to my psyche. Through my stories I hope to educate others, perhaps vicariously extending the healing I've been offered and which I continue to nurture within. But also to instill an appreciation for, and the desire to protect, that complex environment I was blessed to call home.

As Arizona's human population burgeons into the twenty-first century, native habitat will continue to be supplanted by subdivisions preserving none of its original splendor unless we, its caretakers, envision a different future, embody different values and ensure the protection of desert biodiversity.

Come all you lads and lasses,

I'd have you give attention

To these few lines I'm about to write here.

Tis of the four seasons of the year that

I shall mention,

The beauty of all things doth appear.

"The Seasons"

(Traditional nineteenth century English verse)

Spring

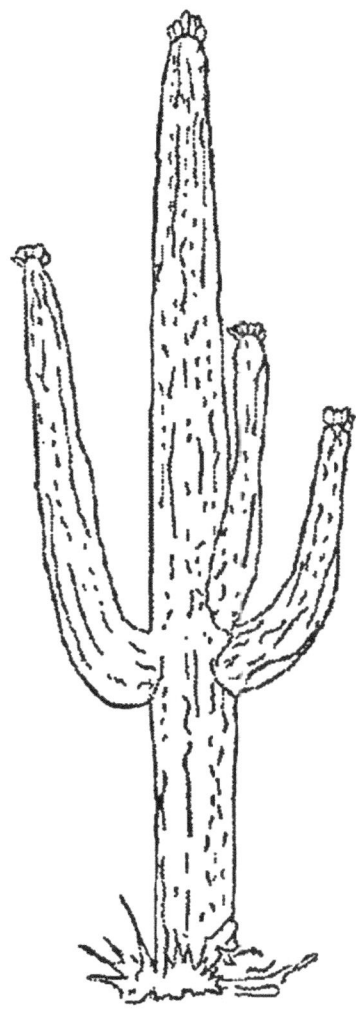

Verdin Drinking

We do love our experts don't we? We have Dr. Phil to cure us of misthoughts, Oprah to spare us misreads, Judge Judy to keep us within the law, fashion experts to keep us from fashion foibles, health experts, exercise experts, diet experts, legal experts, color experts, religious experts, news experts, weather experts, travel experts, nature experts. You name it. We don't want mere students of life. We want experts. Never mind that more often than not those experts pontificate opinions diametrically opposed to other experts in their field. There's security to be found for the non-expert in an expert's advice. And security for the expert in his cadre of believers.

* * * * *

"Mastery," the psychologist said. "That's the ticket to self-esteem. That's the road to success. Master your topic and you're on your way."

"Hmmm," I said, watching him. He was dressed stylishly, perfectly groomed, not a hair misplaced. His office was smartly furnished, glowing with affluence and smelling of polish and new carpet. I was assured by those who recommended him that he was tops in his field. He'd root out the weed of my depression for me, guaranteed.

"That attitude seems profoundly lacking in humility," I interrupted. "Mastery? Who can begin to claim such a thing? Better to bow to the mystery of life. Better to claim nothing beyond the status of eternal student."

"Who told you that?" he asked, before continuing to pontificate on mastery.

I ceased listening and remembered the day I met Verdin. I had recently moved to my rural home in the desert of central Arizona. Raised in the suburbs, I loved the experience of nature up close and personal. I was surprised daily by wonders I'd never imagined. I had so much to learn and was eager to do so.

"What's that little bird on the feeder?" I asked a neighbor. "It has a red chest and face."

"A house finch," she smiled, amused at my lack of knowledge.

I bought a field guide to help me identify the birds.

Later, in the spring heat of mid-afternoon, a bird perched on the bird bath. It was diminutive in size, about half the bulk of a house sparrow. I'd seen it earlier cavorting in the bushes in my courtyard, a midget dynamo in constant motion amongst the leaves, plucking tiny insects invisible to me. I couldn't see its features, though, because it was so intent in its hunting; it never stopped moving long enough to give me a good look. Then it perched on the bird bath and took a drink.

It was gray, primarily, except for its face. That was a bright, sunny yellow. And its shoulder had a rusty-red epaulet.

"Those markings have to be distinctive," I said aloud and went immediately to my field guide, product of bird experts. I scanned the pictures until I found my visitor.

"Evidently getting what little it needs from its diet of insects and seeds, the verdin has never been seen to drink or bathe." So wrote the verdin expert.

But I'd just seen Verdin drinking.

(Evidently Verdin doesn't read. Or can't follow instructions.)

So much for mastery.

I quit my musing and returned my attention to the resident "expert" at hand.

"Verdin told me," I answered the doctor belatedly, interrupting the flow of his lesson plan. "Verdin told me there was no such thing as mastery. And wasn't it Socrates who said something like, 'I only know that I don't know?'"

Me? I choose to retain the capacity for surprise. To know that I don't know. I choose to be the eternal student, not master. I choose the attitude of humility before Mystery-- the mystery of life--the mystery embodied in Verdin.

To hell with mastery.

A Problem of Security

My garden, I hoped, would be a fortress. But I failed in every effort to make it that.

I fenced it round with American Fencing, skirted that with chicken wire, and buried smaller mesh wire six inches underground with six inches still above dirt to reinforce the other two fences. I roofed it all with chicken wire too.

When I planted, and dutifully watered the seeds into bushes, the status of my garden's security was obvious. The only critter that seemed unable to get into it was, perhaps, an elephant, but that may be only because elephants are scarce around my house.

I've watched zucchini plants flower and fruit. (Come on, everybody who plants zucchini winds up begging friends and neighbors to take some off their hands.) Just as mine were getting large enough to make me salivate, bites would appear in the glossy, green squash, multiplying each day until the zucchini had disappeared. How and who was getting past my security system?

I watched from a window overlooking my garden. Antelope squirrels, a rodent commonly mistaken for chipmunks, had learned to climb the chicken wire, like a ladder, to scale its two foot height. Then they popped right through the American Fencing to attend the feast. Whenever my tomatoes, watermelon, or squash began to ripen, they too disappeared. Before long, it was a race. Could I snatch it off the vine before they did?

And birds were not deterred either. Forget sparrows, finches and other small flying folk. I had quail in there. They evidently squeezed themselves to whatever size necessary to wiggle their way into my buffet. Or they came in where the chicken wire ceiling didn't quite meet the American Fencing wall. Nothing got by the wildlife. Any construction flaw was capitalized upon.

Despite the competition, yesterday I actually harvested five small tomatoes. They were just turned red, not really fully ripe, but three were free of any peck or gnaw marks. A miracle!

Hooray for my surprise! Three all for me. Despite the lack of security.

A Lesson in Patience

It took ten years to catch the minstrel in the act. I often heard a trilling call as I went about outdoor chores or walked with the dogs, but my luck at capturing the culprit in the act was nil. I'm serious--ten years I stalked the sound. Was it bird? Insect? Just what? I really had no idea, because every attempt I made to sneak up on it was unsuccessful. Silence reigned when I approached the soloist's scene, with no clue remaining as to who the caller had been.

My desert songster frustrated all my efforts, reminding me that I am not in charge here. The gift of this additional bit of knowledge for my list of life experiences would only come in critter time, not mine--detonating any delusions of grandeur I might have about being in control of anything in my Saguaro-clad environment.

Nature finally delivered my gift of surprise after ten years of waiting. Ten years to practice patience.

One day, I heard the familiar trilling and it was so close that I had to try to sneak a peek at the source. I crept through the courtyard to the open-arched window. Cautiously peering through, I spotted a Harris's Antelope Squirrel perched upright on a great, hulking, prickly staghorn cholla. It stood on its hind legs, snout pointed skyward, white throat rippling in its territorial pronouncement.

A squirrel? That was totally unexpected. But if there is a rule for life, perhaps that's it. Expect the unexpected. The desert always challenges what I think I know. Just when I believe I've learned the rule, life breaks it. Variety is more than the spice of life; it *is* life. "New" is always around the next bend, another teacher, another lesson.

It only took ten years to connect the Antelope Squirrel with his call. I'll never live long enough to know all the desert has to offer. It's better to prepare for surprise. "Expect the unexpected." I'll stay away from investments in rules of behavior and persist in expecting surprise.

It's humbling learning patience, living open to surprise. Very humbling.

But freeing too.

It's boundless.

Amazing.

And it only took ten years to catch the damn squirrel in the act!

Oh yeah.... Right.... Patience.

Owl Clover

One of the most lovely gifts of a rainy spring is the fields of owl clover that burst into purple splendor as the night temperatures begin a warming trend and days lengthen, inviting every seed's gestation. Any turn in the road may open a vista of gentle hills covered with this glory of spring.

Owl clover's green stems and needle-like leaves stand topped with flowers having purple lower and upper lips, the lower lip tipped in white or yellow. Each flower is surrounded by purple bracts up to one inch long. The flowers are arranged in a thick, erect spike, typically one spike per plant. Growing alone, this unique flower is impressive, but in great numbers it's absolutely stunning. Any open area of desert floor, if provided enough moisture, may put on such a display. Often a dirt road will fill with the regal carpet.

The bumble bees savor these nectar stops, perhaps because the spikes are large enough to support their weight. They busily browse and ignore my passage through the field. I step most carefully, doing my best to avoid crushing any flowers underfoot, but the sheer numbers make that task impossible.

And then, the looked for "added bonus,"--an albino amongst the purple horde--dollops of vanilla in an ocean of grape sherbet. Not only a treat for the eye, I'm reminded that variety is the rule of life--and will have its way.

A Most Astounding Thing

I saw a most astounding thing today. A most "unquail-like" thing. I saw nine baby quail, preadolescents, by the look of them. They scuttled from cactus to forbes, from one bit of cover to another, working their way to the bird feeder--nervously flowing across the open spaces.

When I first caught a glimpse of them, I thought it odd that there were no adults. Young quail minus attentive adults? That's most "unquail-like."

I remembered seeing this family some days earlier, the first sighting this year of baby quail, so I rejoiced. They made, with parental supervision, exactly the same run that the chicks made alone today, so the lesson on where to go for food had stuck with the little ones.

What happened to the parents? Surely, nothing short of death would keep them from their charges.

The boldest among the chicks had taken over the leadership roles, continuing the browsing patterns their parents had established.

Hopefully, the parents also had time to teach their offspring of the dangers they would be facing daily: what and who to avoid. Ultimately, though, the chicks' natural instincts would have to provide for their survival.

I wondered whether they could fly yet. That skill would be a great advantage. I decided to watch for them daily, marking their progress when they came in to feed.

* * * * *

Later in the morning, another remarkable event: I walked down the long driveway to the mailbox. Suddenly, a strange sound caught my attention, a popping noise, like static in a high tension electric wire. It seemed to be coming from a nearby wash.

As I crossed the road, I found myself face to face with two roadrunners. We had a brief stand-off, then they were on their way, dashing through the desert.

I scouted the nearby wash to see if I could spot anything there to account for their presence. (I have occasionally seen a solitary roadrunner strolling through the yard, but never heard one talking, and seeing two at once was most unusual. Something was up.)

As I looked up the wash, I again heard that popping, from someplace nearby. This time I was so close that I could tell the sound was superimposed over a low *ooooing* moan. In a tree about ten feet away from me was a third roadrunner, a youngster, nervously watching and objecting vociferously to my presence. As I stared, awed by my close encounter, it leaped down from the tree and raced for cover in the greasewood.

I went back into the house and heated a cup of cranberry juice to sip while I pondered my roadrunner experience.

In all my years of living in the desert, I had never been blessed to hear roadrunner chatter before. Then too, I'd never seen parents with a youngster before. So why the sudden roadrunner population explosion?

As I sat outdoors with my drink, two roadrunners dashed through the yard, heading for the bird feeder. My dog saw them and gave chase. Unable to run fast enough to escape, both birds went into glide mode and sailed over to the neighbor's house.

They were gone for now, but I remembered that a local resident once told me that baby quail are quite a delicacy in a roadrunner's spring diet.

The orphaned quail just might be the reason the roadrunners were so numerous today.

For me, sighting so many roadrunners was an astounding thing, but--for the quails, ominous.

Death And Sainthood

I n my capacity as Treasurer on the Board of Directors for our homeowner's association, I collected the bills. This put me in the position of having to speak to other residents about subjects that made us all uncomfortable, like past-due accounts, Small Claims Court, or putting liens on their property.

While I was always willing to work out partial payment plans and do my best to make it easier for my past-due neighbors to get current on their debts, I'm sure some still saw me as the "bad guy" and took no delight in seeing me coming.

As a board member, I was also likely to hear everybody's grievances. There were always complaints about how the board conducted business, and I heard them all as I delivered bills or made collection phone calls and visits.

My point is, since I was both bill collector and a board member, it's possible I saw only the worst aspects of some neighbors. None of us is perfect, least of all me.

One middle-aged man, who lived a half mile from me, was particularly abrasive. I never had to deal with him wearing my bill collector's hat, but when I did visit for any sort of board business, I found him to be a real Type-A personality: a self-made man and his own number one fan.

I watched the interaction between himself and his wife, feeling distinctly thrilled it was she that had to live with him and not me. I found his manner towards her demeaning, though I knew she kept the books for his two businesses and was both witty and attractive, deserving his respect, not criticism. As I discussed association business, he interrupted me and spoke loudly to drown out any point I was trying to make when he disagreed with me. I always left his house hoping to never visit again. Did I just catch him on a bad day? Because it happened more than once, I doubt it.

Type-A that he was, I was not surprised to learn he'd suffered one heart attack before he and his wife built their home and moved out to their rural acreage. His potential for longevity was reinforced for me, however, when I also heard of an encounter he had in his garage one day while working on his car. He thought he heard something, scootched out from under the car, and found himself looking up into the nasal passages of a huge, longhorn steer. The man bellowed. The steer bellowed--then decided to take his curiosity elsewhere. The confrontation was over just that fast, but I was convinced if that occasion didn't deliver my neighbor a second heart attack, nothing would.

I was wrong.

When I went to offer my condolences to his wife, she had buried him just the day before. Since I was also a widow, I knew how overwhelming initial reactions and red tape could be. All she had to say was what a warm, wonderful guy he was, with lots of friends who would miss him so terribly much. Such a saint! Everyone who knew him, loved him.

Everyone but me, I thought.

So who was that dude I dealt with each time I came visiting? Obviously not the one she'd buried.

I've seen this before--the deceased get eulogized in larger than life terms. But how are they really remembered by those that knew them? Only for the good? If the dead man and the one I'd known were the same, then I can only reach one deduction.

Don't bother striving to develop any noble or humanitarian qualities, living by Golden Rule, etc. To achieve sainthood--just die.

Update

I still see the orphaned quail chicks because they come around the feeder each morning. Older now, they look teen-aged. Their numbers are down to five. I'm amazed there are still so many left.

What a lesson they are in determination, reminding me that life tends to find a way, even faced with enormous odds. At the same time, their absent siblings remind me that death is part of life, not its opposite.

The survivors are no longer little-chick-cute, but not yet endowed with the colors and grace of adulthood either. Gawky adolescents, their topknots are developing normally, but look hilarious, too stringy and thin to be taken seriously.

Since I spot them each morning, I call them "The Breakfast Bunch."

I watch while they scurry from bursage to creosote, clucking to each other in single file to hide behind this plant, and that bunch of grass, gradually working their way to the feeder. They wouldn't be quail if they weren't eternally conversing with one another.

I cross my fingers and throw up a prayer for their safety during the day and that they retain their numbers on the morrow.

Penis Envy

I confess. I have a classic case of penis envy. Freud was right about us women.

I didn't know enough to have this problem as a kid. Our family went camping, but we never really roughed it. We generally stayed in campgrounds that had bathroom and shower facilities. It wasn't until I moved to the country that I had cause to become envious.

It all began the first time I left home to go on a long walk without having emptied my bladder first. Yes, I was trained to potty before leaving home, but obviously not well-trained.

Sometimes I misjudge my ability to get home again before bladder overload becomes an issue, but fortunately, my hikes away from toilets take me into the privacy of the great outdoors, *sans* many humans. Usually, when nature calls, I can just squat and answer.

Even with all the practice I've had over the years, I've never developed a technique that leaves my shoes out of it-- out of the stream, sure, but not out of the splatter.

Oh, I've experimented. Thinking that perhaps a gentler, though longer period of flow would cut down on splatter, I've tried slowing the stream to a trickle, which takes enormous willpower on a full bladder. It was hard to tell whether the results equaled success. While there was less splatter in the moment, flow time was increased, so splatter time was too.

Next I tried exerting myself to create the most forceful stream possible, thinking perhaps a shorter time of flow would ultimately splash less, but more splash for less time was no solution either.

Whatever the effects of flow time or stream force, I at least had the comfort of a relieved bladder, but it was still irritating knowing men never had to deal with splattered shoes. Even more annoying--men can make a game of it all.

My son, when a boy, derived great elation from taking his first pee of the morning while standing at the garage door, shooting his stream as far down the driveway as possible. I counseled against his anti-social behavior, preparing him for the day he might find himself living in suburbia, but he continued his experiment with unabated glee.

Deep down, I must admit, I envied his abilities. For me, range could never even be an issue.

And what really pissed me off--so to speak--was the story my neighbor told me of the day she went out to her garage to find her three-year-old son dashing around, joyfully squirting the cats. To be able to aim at and hit a moving target is just too much!

I'm consumed with envy.

Scorpion Sneaking

To kill or not to kill. That is the question.

In my studies and journeys with fellow nature enthusiasts, I often find folks with a no-kill policy. Nothing should ever be killed, simply removed and relocated--be it bug or bobcat. I respect that philosophy, though I don't always live by it.

In my rural life style, I've often come across lifelong ranchers, farmers and neighbors who feel quite differently. One, who has lost a number of calves to coyotes and gardens to varmints, says, "The only folks who believe no one should ever kill anything have never made their living off the desert." I can respect his attitude too, though I choose not to put out rat poison to get rid of the woodrats in my yard. (I might, though, if one were eating all the wiring in my truck, which is the current concern of a neighbor. He is evidently breeding some sort of Super-Rat, because the one in his truck polishes off whole boxes of rat poison, kicks the empty box out from under the hood of the vehicle, as if calling for room service, and adds on to rat headquarters down by the air filter, all with no apparent ill-effects from the poison.)

My philosophy? Well, I guess it's somewhere in the middle.

I really don't like bugs in my house. Outside, they're fine, but my house is off limits. I have no problem smacking crickets, and will relocate scorpions and spiders if it is convenient. If there is any risk of sting or bite, however, I'm ready with the fly swatter.

Living where I do, I'm bound to have a few unwelcome visitors from time to time. Once I had a small snake. I threw a pillow case over it to blind it, then picked it up and put it outside. Mostly my unwelcome guests are in the bug category, though. Or arachnid.

Once I went to the kitchen at night. I didn't turn on the light, as the dim lighting from the other room let me see enough to get a glass of water. Then I noticed the scrub pad, which sat on the edge of the sink, seemed to be fraying, though it was fairly new. I turned on the light to investigate and spotted a huge scorpion perched on top of the pad--so large it must have knocked to get in. That shook me up a bit. That scorpion didn't live much longer.

Most likely, the one that snuck in the kitchen door while I was holding it open for a dog to enter, the one I watched slip behind the kitchen cabinets before I could do anything about it, will suffer the same fate when it reappears. Even though I hold all life forms sacred, I refuse to share my house with all of them. All scorpions are on the "Not Welcome" list. In nature, everything has its place, but my place is not necessarily its place.

Joseph Campbell, after years of studying myth and the cultures that birthed them, postulated that the reality of living is that life destroys life in order to continue life. No life form is exempt. That realization tore ancient human psyches apart with grief and guilt. Perhaps also with insecurity, for what could guarantee that more life would be available in the future to sustain human life? Religion and ritual developed, Campbell says, to assuage the pain and acknowledge the debt.

There really is nothing new under the sun. Though life and death are ultimately one, both springing from the same force, call it God or whatever, we live in a world where they appear to be opposites. Our cave-dwelling forefathers had to develop some way of balancing life and death, and so must we.

As far as I'm concerned, the scorpion behind the kitchen cabinets better stay there or else.

"To kill, or not to kill. That is the question."

Two Bees Attacking

When I built the house, I chose oak exterior doors. I had them stained and varnished a dark walnut color. What a maintenance headache those doors turned out to be! Every six months I was re-varnishing. Over the years, I tried many products, but man has not made the sealant that can stand up to the desert sun. It was during one of my regular maintenance varnishings that I made the acquaintance of two memorable bees.

Spring's abundance of flowers in years of good winter rains means the wild honey bees will be dividing their colonies. New queens will hatch, taking flight with subjects intent on establishing new wax castles in new nook and cranny realms. Each spring I watch in fearful fascination as swarms pass overhead. I'm not so much afraid of the swarm as where they intend to set up housekeeping.

Words can't describe the experience of a swarm on the move. It starts with the low hum of the insect legion's approach and increases in volume as the bees pass overhead, then diminishes as they continue their journey. The dark, synchronized cloud moves with one intent, one communal mind. It's an awesome sight.

Each spring, I watch for the scouts around my house. I know that single bees that are intent on cracks in walls and small holes in woodwork instead of flowering plants are scouts checking for potential homesites. If possible, I squirt a dose of bug spray into the place they find interesting to discourage them and convince them to move on, but luck is not always with me. I have a well-used beekeeper's business card on hand and call him as soon as I see evidence of a hive's activity.

One time a colony moved into the attic through a small hole in the stucco. The constant bee traffic under the eaves and honey oozing onto a windowsill clued me in to their presence. That hive had to be destroyed, as the queen could not be recovered and without her, her subjects were going nowhere. Destroying a hive disappoints the beekeeper. He'd much rather gain a colony for his honey enterprise, which puts his kids through college.

The scenarios he likes to find are ones where the swarms settle into a bush or tree, gathering into football sized-and-shaped clumps, resting for the night, or perhaps an hour or two, before moving on to a permanent location. I've had a number of those buzzing baubles in my bushes over the years. Then, the beekeeper can easily smoke them, box the queen, and collect the colony. He uses a smudge pot to deliver the smoke, which makes the bees groggy and manageable. He always uses hat and face screen to protect his head and neck from stings, but I've never seen him suit up completely.

One time I had a colony move into a wall of my house, entering and exiting through a crack in a false scupper. That colony kept things interesting.

At night they could be heard buzzing behind outlet covers and light switch plates, trying to follow the light. Eventually, they did find a way into the house through a bathroom fan vent. We went from a two to a one-bathroom house immediately. I sealed off the room the bees claimed by closing the door and stuffing towels against the bottom edge. The beekeeper had his own spot on my speed-dial that spring, as I kept him appraised of the bees progress until he could get out to us.

In the meantime, the bees and I went about our business. They collected pollen and made honey in the hive they formed in the wall of my house. I began yet another door re-varnishing project. I was working twenty feet from their front hive entrance, but I was not within sight of them and wasn't doing anything I thought might provoke them. I didn't anticipate any problem and had none the first day.

But the second day, two bees took offense at my handiwork and attacked me. Actually, I'm grateful only two decided to shut down my jobsite. One stung me in the shoulder and the other stung the hell out of the cloth I used to swing at them as they zeroed in on me. I have no idea what set them off--what I did differently from the day before.

Afterwards, I was angry, and baffled by their behavior. When the beekeeper finally got a hole in his hectic, bee-collecting schedule to come out to my house, he had to destroy the colony. There was no way he could get the queen.

An embedded stinger and my welt ensured there'd be no remorse on my part. Only the beekeeper mourned their passing.

Dress Clothes in the Desert

He shot my dog when his went into heat and my yellow lab went to pay a visit.

That lab was the most beautiful, laid-back and easy-going dog you could ever ask to meet.

When we first picked him up at the pound, I gave my son permission to name our handsome pup whatever he wanted, and much to my horror, he chose "Arf."

When Arf came up missing, I had no idea where he'd gone; he just wasn't home when I got back from work. I would have tied him up for the time the female was in menses, had I been told of his visits, but I did not realize my young dog now considered himself adult enough to seek out girlfriends.

My neighbor, who lived 2 miles away and the owner of the female, partied with friends one night until drunk, then decided to use my dog for target practice. Months later I found out what happened, when others heard he was missing, found the carcass, and told me....

* * * * *

My dog's killer was known for being drunk and disorderly. Patrons of the local bar regretted his almost

34

nightly attendance because he always drank until he was a rowdy, mean drunk. He frequently brought one of his dogs along, a dog he expected to sit beside him in the bar. God help that dog if it went over to sniff someone, or was friendly toward anyone else. That was a crime punished by a vicious kicking. His dog was to be attentive to no one but him.

When drunk, he picked fights at the drop of a hat with anyone who offended him by word or deed. A true redneck, he was a regular and colorful addition to any gathering at the bar.

He worked as the hired hand at a local ranch which had once been large, but had been split and sold down to just 10 acres. This left approximately 15 animals to tend, four or five of which were pigs, expressly forbidden in the restrictions governing our homeowner's association.

He tended the ranch for the owner, who worked and lived in town. She resented the fact that newcomers were moving into the area, and he shared her attitude. He threatened to shoot anyone who came onto her property or used the road running beside it.

"It's a private road," he said. "We have proof, and trespassers will be shot."

He carried his gun openly, and regularly threatened to use it.

He slept with the boss's teenaged daughter in the ranch house, rough quarters with dirt floors. Neither cleanliness nor godliness was familiar territory since they had no modern amenities except electricity. Especially in the summer, he had a distinct aroma.

He enjoyed snagging part-time jobs as an extra in any movie shooting in the valley, particularly westerns. The rest of us called him "The Marlboro Man," because he dressed like the stereotypical cowboy, black hat, pointy-toed boots, bandana around his neck, sporting several days' worth of beard.

* * * * *

She was a neighbor who raised a jobless husband and two preteen girls in a crowded garage stuffed with furniture from her previous home in town. There was barely room for the four of them to turn around. It was constant chaos, but that was all that could be afforded for the present. The house would be built later.

Later--when her husband had a job again.

Later--when he would take some responsibility for the girls and the horses again.

Later--when he could stop obsessing about the job from which he had been laid off and begin to support his family again.

She was feeling the burden of being her family's sole financial provider. She was angry because, in her mind, her husband was not trying hard enough to get another job. He was being picky, and they could not afford "picky."

They fought often.

She worked each day at her girls' school cafeteria. She always wore a nice, long-sleeved blouse, slacks and pair of dress shoes. That made her, she felt, appropriately professional.

It wasn't her habit to change her clothes when she got home before doing chores or walking in the desert, her chosen form of exercise. She was concerned about her weight and walked for miles in her good clothes through the desert around our neighborhood, often stopping to visit me for a glass of water and a little chat, spilling out her frustrations. She sweated profusely in those clothes; shorts and a tank top would have been much cooler. By the time she got to my house, she was very thirsty. I asked her why she walked in her work clothes, which covered up so much of her body and must have been hot.

"Helps to take off the water weight," she said.

* * * * *

The weather was hot, unseasonably so that year. It was only May, but already temperatures were 115 degrees. Usually we work up to that heat gradually, later in the summer, but that particular May had no mercy. Even so, she still walked--after work on weekdays, early in the morning on weekends, trying to shed those extra pounds and perhaps some of her worries.

When I first heard that her husband had reported her missing, I didn't think much of it. Probably they had argued and she took off on one of her long walks, perhaps visiting with friends along her way, not caring if he was worried because she was still angry.

The next day a search party was formed: some set out on horseback, some overhead in a plane, some on foot.

Marlboro Man was one of those on horseback. He and a mounted friend were the ones who found her, lying face-up in a wash, dead of dehydration and exposure, her arm up over her blackened face as if to ward off the relentless sun.

She was wearing her work clothes.

* * * * *

Years later I was out walking, one of my own long, sanity-restoring walks in the desert. I was recently home from work and still wearing my slacks, a long sleeved blouse and dress shoes. I heard an ATV coming along the road behind me, still invisible around a curve. Preferring not to be run over in a surprise encounter, I moved off the road and a little way up a wash. As he drew near, I saw the driver was Marlboro Man.

He stopped when he saw me, cut the engine, and asked if I was OK. I said I was fine, just out with the dogs before calling it a day. He told me how seeing me all dressed up reminded him of a woman who had died of exposure out here some years back and how finding her had really bothered him. It was something he could not forget, so he had to stop to be sure I was OK before going on his way.

You could have knocked me over with a feather! Who would have guessed Marlboro Man to be the sort who would give our neighbor's death a second thought? Not I. I couldn't imagine him spending a single moment lying awake at night thinking about it. But he obviously had.

This aspect of his character wasn't one I'd ever seen before. Talk about surprises!

Update 2

I have not seen the orphaned quail for a week now.

Summer

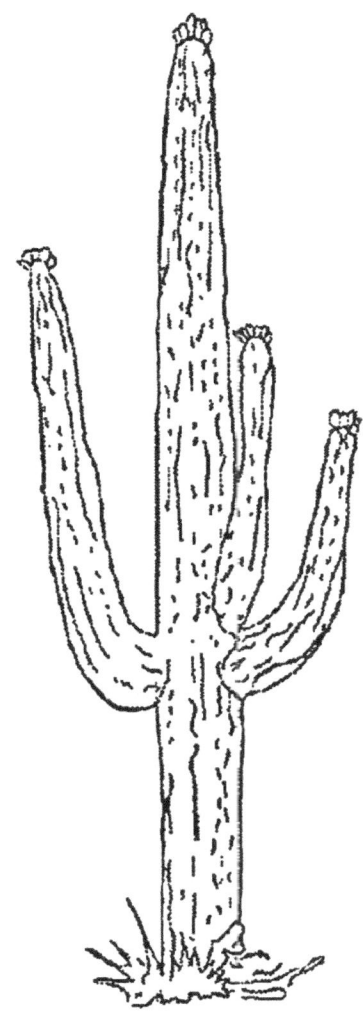

Sidewinder Coiled

The morning coolness was giving way to the sun, which hung just behind the mountains on the horizon. As that blazing orb peeked over the jagged edge of the earth, the intensity of its heat and light hit me head on, promising extreme conditions later in the day.

Early summer is like that; the mornings still blessedly cool. It's the best time to be outside, for both my dogs and myself, the best time to comfortably cover the miles we walk for daily exercise.

Another pleasure of early mornings is that they are still unbleached. Morning colors are crisp and well-delineated; they vibrate with clarity. Later the sun's severity will strip deep hues from the land and sky, washing everything earthbound a dusty beige, and the sky a thin white-blue.

This morning's first light, however, still offered up a liquid-azure sky, sharp shadows marking hills from valleys in the mountains, a greener green to the palo verde's trunk and a brighter gold to the fuzzy-blossomed catclaw acacia.

The dogs were off scouting the trail for ground squirrels, rabbits, quail, lizards, or anything else crackling through the dried grasses and forbes beneath trees or bushes. That growth, the residual from the spring's population of annuals, rustled with every breeze or creature moving through it, greatly inciting the dogs. Even the smallest horned toad sounded like an elephant when it waddled through the brittle memorials of life in kinder days.

With the dogs busy, I was left with my own thoughts.

When the path turned north, I gave thanks to have the rising sun out of my eyes. Spared the frontal attack of light, this new direction seemed full of grace, at least as far as my eyes were concerned.

I settled into a comfortable pace, absentmindedly strolling, until I was caught up short by the sight of a two-foot-long Sidewinder rattlesnake.

I instinctively stiffened with alarm, then noticed the neatly coiled snake was quite relaxed. Snoozing, in fact. My trail mate was nestled into a depression in the sand, meditating in the gentle morning breezes. Its pattern of color blended perfectly with the browns and gravels of the rocky trail. What had caught my eye before I could step on it was the neat coil of its design motif, the spiral standing out from the more linear surroundings.

It never stirred; never was it aware of my presence. I was free to cautiously admire it. The horns over the eyes ID'd it for me. I almost wished I could see it in motion--that odd, sideways, slip-sliding style of movement it's named for, but I liked it better in snooze-mode. I circled around it and continued my journey.

The encounter remained in my mind the rest of the day, for I was quite severely startled out of complacency.

Danger, I was reminded, slept in sandy pits in my trail, impressive, even at rest. I idly wondered what sort of imprint it would leave in the soil embracing it. It would have to be as perfectly round as the coiled reptile I'd seen, wouldn't it? I decided to check it out by coming by the same spot later.

Even as I put more distance between myself and the snake, I dwelt on the potential menace it represented. Inattentiveness could be costly. I was reminded not to take my morning bliss for granted. I didn't have to stretch my imagination far to see this slumbering fellow rattling his tail, coiled with a different intent, striking out at the perceived danger I represented. The more I thought about it, the more unnerved I got, gladder and gladder I'd left the critter to its dreaming.

I still went back later, though.

As twilight gathered, with the sun tucked behind the western horizon, I sought out the snake's napping place, knowing the reptile would have been driven away by the day's heat. I searched the dust of the path for the snake's imprint.

Nothing. Nothing could be found of the morning's menace.

Maybe the day's breezes had blown away the evidence? I couldn't even find the slither marks that would indicate the snake's path of retreat from whatever disturbed its sleep. No sign whatsoever the viper was ever there.

I left, wondering how many other of my fears might disappear with a little passing time and a breath of wind.

Even with such a perfect, surprising example of that principle before me, I have a hard time trusting.

I'm bound to outlive the preponderance of my anxieties, but fear still has a home in me. Fear I won't have enough health, enough money, enough love, enough strength, enough wit and wile, enough enough.

(What an odd word, "enough." And let's hang whoever decided to spell it like that.)

So, what about those "enough" vipers?

They, too, shall pass.

Beau's Death

One thing I've always appreciated about the desert in summer--its honesty. It reminds constantly of its power to deliver death at the slightest error of judgment. I appreciate its directness. I'm more aware of the risk I take in venturing forth into it. I appreciate my time with it more deeply. I've had to develop a sort of peaceful acceptance of death, because its presence is almost, but not quite, hidden within the scorching desert landscape.

For fourteen plus years I had a golden retriever--or rather, he had me.

We got Beau at two months of age, and he was exactly four months older than our son, Pat. My husband thought he would train Beau for the show circuit, eventually building him up to championship status.

I only knew *I* wasn't tackling that task.

I figured that my husband would never get around to it either. He was in the Navy, a pilot, and simply not home long enough to accomplish such a long-term project.

He condemned Beau to show circuit obscurity when he died in a plane crash. Anticipating a recruiting job, stationed in Phoenix where he would be one of two pilots who traveled to out-of-state college campuses, we had moved to a rental house in that desert metropolis. Chip went to Florida to recruitment school and to retrain in single-engine aircraft. He had been flying P-3's, a four-engined submarine hunter, and needed to be re-certified in the smaller plane he'd be flying out of Phoenix. He and his instructor pilot were both killed when their aircraft crashed and burned while practicing touch-and-goes on a little airstrip outside of Fairhope, Alabama. Our son was 15 months old, and Beau 19 months.

The long-suffering dog was my son's primary playmate until preschool. It was grueling duty which included eye exams, pulled ears, squirts from the hose and use as a pillow. Beau would endure until he could take no more, then lumber off to another location, hoping that "out of sight" would mean "out of mind."

There were paybacks, though. My son had a special blanket. That blanket went everywhere my son went for the first four years of his life. The blanket began life white, with a white satin binding. It wound up a rag, no satin in sight, and white only briefly when under the recent influence of bleach.

Beau gleefully played his part in the blanket demolition. Whenever we returned home in the car, that blanket was Beau's target. He would snatch it out of my son's arms as Pat sat, still strapped in the car seat, helpless in the tug of war with the much stronger dog.

My son's role was to scream in protest. If I did not play my part and instantly drop everything to rescue the blanket, Beau would stop running around with it and tear it up instead.

It was a daily drama upon our return home from preschool and work, and the only distraction that could save the blanket was a paper cup, so we often stopped at Circle K and bought a drink which we finished by the time we reached home. Beau would rip that cup to smithereens, leaving the blanket alone, and thus avoid the scolding to which he was mostly immune anyway.

As my son grew up, the blanket was put away in a dresser drawer. Beau, though, never outgrew his paper cup fetish.

Our retriever remained forever a puppy, at least mentally. He drove guests crazy demanding their attention, practically crawling onto their laps if they dared to overlook him.

Ignoring him was a strategy doomed to failure, because Beau was really good at ensuring he got attention. Male visitors, who tried to slip by without stopping to pet him before heading into the house, got a nose in the crotch they did not soon forget. Women who did not greet and pet him would not be allowed to pass, no matter how many attempts they made to move by him and reach the door. Little children who visited were usually terrified of the huge dog charging over to love them, whose wild greetings typically succeeded in knocking them down.

Calm was not in Beau's personality. If we laughed or yelled, he was instantly alongside, demanding attention, wanting to be part of whatever you were excited about. If you sat down, his face was in your face, insisting he be petted. Only putting him outside broke that cycle, but then he was at the arcadia door, leaving wet nose prints and pawing to be let in.

He was difficult and stubborn, even dog school didn't help. One instructor said that Beau was a dog who was a leader, would have been the alpha male in a pack, and that perfect obedience would not be his strong suit. But he had a good heart and was loyal to a fault. The trainer's assessment was right on the money.

Once, my son and I were riding our bikes, attended by our dogs, who were exploring nearby. Suddenly, three Australian Shepherds ran out from a house we were passing, growling and stalking us, stiff-legged, fur standing upright along their spines.

In rushed Beau to the rescue! After about 30 seconds of growling, the fight was on.

Three against Beau. Beau won. Two were whipped right away and fled for home, but he nearly killed the last one. Beau had it by the throat, strangling it. The dog's owner and I had to physically pull the two dogs apart. Beau would never consider biting a person, but a dog threatening his family would be dealt with in no uncertain terms.

While he did not grow up--he did grow old. Eventually his hindquarters gave him grief and his hips weakened to the point that I had to help him up whenever he lay down in even a slight depression in the ground. He could manage alone if the ground was level. When it was not, he would make little yipping sounds as his way of calling for help when he wanted to get up.

He was so determined not to be left at home when the other dogs and I started down the driveway on our evening walks, that he would force himself to come. His hind legs would lose strength every five or six steps, causing a stumble, but he never went down, and he never gave up, so I shortened the walks to suit his capabilities--at the end, a mere 1/4 mile. No more the five-mile-walks of his younger days.

Twice in his life he decided he just could not manage any walk at all. There he sat in the driveway watching us leave, pathetic longing showing in his face. He waited there until our return, the arthritis just too much to bear.

Beau died in June. June is summer in the desert, not early summer, but full blast summer, and pre-monsoon too. With the monsoon, the increase in humidity lowers the temperatures somewhat, but the monsoons do not come until July.

I left Beau outside with the other dogs because I was going to be gone all day. Had I been gone less than the full day, I would have left him in the house, but I did not know if his ancient bladder could handle being there all day, and having an accident in the house embarrassed him terribly. Outside, the dogs had their wading pool as well as buckets of water, and they moved with the shade to keep comfortable.

On this particular June day, after we left home, Beau had parked himself in the planter in the shade, where the soil was still wet from the last watering, the coolest spot he could find. Unfortunately, it was not at all level.

When we got home, around 6:00 P.M. we found Beau dead of exposure, still in the planter, which by that time was in the full sun and had been for about four hours. He had not been able to get up for shade or water, and no one had been home to hear the yipping barks he was undoubtedly making, calling for someone to come out and rescue him.

My son and I were stunned. A rush of pain and shock swept us both away. Then, together, we picked up Beau's golden-red body and, too late to be of any help to him, carried him to a spot in the shade.

We buried Beau on the east side of the house, taking turns with the pickax and shovel until we had the hole deep enough. The effort required was somehow an outlet for our grief. I knew it even at the time. We then covered the grave with logs from the woodpile to keep the coyotes from digging into it.

For the first time, I understood my father's response to the phone call telling him of his mother's nearness to death in a hospital nearly two thousand miles away. He simply hung up the phone and went out to mow the grass. My mother phoned to make his reservation for the plane trip back to Chicago. I was almost ten years old, and mystified by my dad's sudden need to mow the lawn. After burying Beau, I understood how the physical work of mowing, in the days before power or gas mowers, helped him sublimate his grief.

I struggled briefly with guilt, but upon reflection, I knew Beau and Death were ready for each other. It was time. I would have chosen other circumstances, had I been able to foresee the future, but I could not. I instinctively knew that I could waste energy beating myself up for the course of events I never intended, or I could refuse to do that to myself and take a step toward peace. I chose peace.

The desert's intense June sun has no regard for age or arthritic hips. Not in man or beast. It kills for the smallest mistake in judgment. It simply is what it is.

Like Death.

Ultimately, beyond our control.

And honest.

Update 3

There are only two quail that make the trip to the bird feeder each morning. It is possible The Breakfast Club changed their feeding pattern and come to the yard at a different time of day, but I don't think that too likely. Either the two young adult quail are the last of the orphans, the only two to survive, or they are a mated pair. It is impossible to know for sure.

I enjoy thinking that two of the ten orphans made it to adulthood. I know this isn't likely. I know the odds were against them. Still, I believe I recognize these two and that they continue the feeding circuit ten began.

After all--stranger things have happened. Miracles occur. I choose to believe two made it.

Phoebeville

Early this spring I had a pair of Say's phoebes inspect my garage for its possibilities as a nesting site. I don't know who decided the issue--probably the female--but the next thing I knew, a bird was flying back and forth, regularly depositing construction materials on top of the garage door opener.

Say's phoebes are about six inches long, have black tails, gray backs and wings, and a rouge tinge to their bellies. Both sexes look exactly alike, so I never could tell who took on what duties during the nest building stage of their occupancy. Obviously, they can tell the difference, which accounts for the population increase each spring. Regardless of who built it, within days, the grass flying into the garage was woven into a neat, tidy custard cup-sized bowl, with bits of pepper plant intermittently inserted to break up the monotony.

Then she began sitting.

Every time my son or I went into the garage from the kitchen, probably the most used door in the house, Mom would spook off the nest and alight in the mesquite nearby, watching and waiting for us to finish our business before taking up her station again. We felt bad about constantly disturbing her, but we soon learned if we did not look directly at her as we came out the door, she would sit tight, convinced we didn't know she was there. Silly, yes, but it was the mutually agreed upon game that allowed her the bliss of feeling safe. Periodically, she would leave the nest to go snag a dragonfly or whatnot out of mid-air to keep up her strength. This is why I think she did all the nest-time duty. She still had to supply her own meals. Dad was nowhere to be seen, but was undoubtedly nearby. On one meal-break I climbed into the back of the truck in an effort to see into the nest, but couldn't see in well enough to tell if it housed any eggs. I reached in gently and lightly touched a single egg. I hoped Mom wouldn't be upset with me and abandon the nest, but that was never to prove a problem throughout the proceedings. My presence was occasionally disruptive, but not a serious hindrance to the project at hand--or wing.

Normally, I left the garage door open while I was home, except at night. My familiar routine had to be chucked to comply with my new tenant's schedule, however. One night I forgot about her and closed the door while she was out hunting. I feared the night without her warmth had finished off the eggs, which were three in number by then, but the next morning, she took her position again as soon as I opened the garage up and carried on as usual. I resigned myself to not using the garage door, leaving it up even when away from home, so that she might continue her project unhindered. Sure enough, all three eggs hatched and a bug parade began as both parents scuttled in and out in a ceaseless effort to still the three demanding voices I could hear, but not see, within the grass and feather-lined splendor of the nest.

About a week later I started to see three faces peeking over the nest's rim, watching for the next airborne meal. Mom and Dad were sufficiently shy that they would not come into the garage with their deliveries while I was watching. They sat in the mesquite making their mournful warning cry until I left, informing the kids of danger and warning them to keep a low profile. This they did, most dutifully. They would hunker down, at the first warning from their parents, flattening themselves as much as possible into the nest and holding perfectly still until Mom and Dad arrived to show the danger had passed.

The stream of insects was endless, beginning at the crack of dawn and continuing until deepening dusk. Meanwhile, the voices became larger, the nestlings did too, feathers developed, crowding became a concern, and the youngsters left headquarters to perch on the garage door opener. There they bobbled for position in the lineup where Mom and Dad could feed them.

Waste disposal was a wonder. There was a coordinated plan that differed each night. One night my vehicle would get baptized, the next night my son's. Everyone, apparently, agreed to hang together in leaving their deposits in one spot only. The rhyme or reason for the rotation of evacuation points was beyond me. I suspect it was intentional, but probably not personal.

Two months later, my guests began making test flights. Now I never knew where I might find a young aviator--atop the broom, perched on the bike, fluttering at the window? The kids all made the same mournful warning sound as their parents until I left. The adults made quick, darting flights of panic just outside the garage to distract me from their offspring, still not trusting me completely.

About this time, I began speculating with delight on the empty nest syndrome. I couldn't wait to get my garage back. Surely they would soon be on their way. The kids spent most of the day outside, practicing short flights between nearby trees and creosote bushes, perching to wait for Mom and Dad's meal delivery service. Each night, though, they returned to the confines of the garage to huddle together on the garage door opener.

The day finally came when the whole crew was out for the day and didn't return to home base for the night. One more day, I thought. I'll give them one more day to be sure they are off on their own. Then the garage is mine.

The next day Mom began sitting again, resulting in four more eggs. The chick-rearing process began again, ending successfully, once again. The newest four are putting in their flight hours, developing the skills which will soon have them feeding themselves and finding other quarters.

It's been a great learning experience, but I want my garage back. Though I will always fondly recall this year's seven offspring and hope to meet them again hunting my land; after four months of Phoebeville in my parking space, I'm ready for a break.

Oh my God. She won't go for a third round--will she? It's June and summer is upon us. She won't go for three, will she?

Lessons From The Local Tavern

I tend to forget just how many verdins live in the desert, until summertime. The season's relentless heat causes that bird, and many other diurnal critters to congregate in places of shade, most particularly in places of shade and water. The rest of the year they are scattered hither and yon throughout the desert, but not summer.

The verdin's quick "chip-chipping" is a common accompaniment to my morning walks. They flit in the wolfberry bushes lining washes, darting after tiny insects visible to them alone, chattering to one another, playing tag from bush to tree, ever in constant motion. They simply *are* perpetual movement. They probably flutter in their sleep.

But come afternoon, they're in my courtyard, scouring the oleander for crawling munchies, rocking the hummingbird feeder to sip the nectar, or clinging to window edges for cool drafts of air leaking from my house. My patio is then a local watering hole, a neighborhood "wild kingdom" tavern.

The verdins are far outnumbered by the house sparrows. The latter are bigger, bulkier, wallow in water bowls, squabble over sunflower seeds, jostle against the house together, chatter noisily, are more dependent on human beings for food and shelter and native to Europe, not the desert. In my courtyard, though, they dominate.

I often feel similarly outnumbered.

I was "at home" with the concept of reincarnation when I first read about it as a ten-year-old, even though when I questioned her, my mother told me that was something *some* people believed in, but not us. I knew then that whatever I was, I was not an "us."

Further exploration showed me a new take on the conflict between good and evil, very much a part of my Christian upbringing. Of far greater relevance to me was the Hindu/Buddhist/Tao perspective where evil was understood as ignorance. Not knowing the interconnection of all things was the root of that.

This change in perspective turned the world and human psyche from a war zone where good and evil were constantly trying to overcome one another to a place of learning interwoveness. For me, life's not a matter of stomping out evil, ego or negativity so much as balancing it against the greater wisdom of increasing awareness of interconnectedness.

The verdin, I've noticed, is never anything but itself. No matter how outnumbered it is by the house sparrows. Mine is the lesson in that, and mine is the continuing journey of self-discovery.

The Spider and the Ant

I t really is a fine art--letting go.

Yesterday I sat on a bench, warming in the sun. The early morning temperature was still cool, with the wind skittering through the mesquite bosque just enough to intensify cool into cold in the shady spots. The bench was astride a busy anthill, so I watched them at work. They were big and black. Slider lizards moved among them, each oblivious to the other. I was surprised because I thought the lizards would consider the ants an entree, but no. They nosed under leaves and rocks in search of other prey.

I noticed an ant dangling in mid-air, hanging from a blade of grass. I thought perhaps it had climbed there in search of seed, then gotten caught in a spider's web, though no distinct web was visible. No spider either. I watched its desperate struggle, thinking that such herculean efforts were sure to wake the spider to the ant's presence, but still saw nothing on the blade of grass but the ant. It appeared the ant's exertions were only getting him more entangled, so I plucked up a straw and scraped him out of his hangman's noose and down to the ground, a trip of three inches.

It was then I finally saw the spider. It had been there all along on the blade of grass, probably adding more strands of web to the ant's burden, but it was so small, not a quarter the size of the ant. It's body was white and its fine yellow legs so thin they were almost invisible.

When I released the ant, the spider wasted not a moment in regret. It simply scrambled to the top of a nearby rock and sent out streamers of webbing that connected it to another blade of grass in line with the anthill's harvesting mission, then began manipulating the new lines into a trap for yet another hapless victim.

The ant, meanwhile, was still entangled, still vulnerable. But the spider let it go, focusing on the new trap. I used my straw several times to help the ant break out of its invisible chains. I separated it from the bits of matter that clung to the webbing it dragged behind, lightening its load. Eventually, with its efforts and mine, it could walk unhindered enough to leave the scene. I didn't see that, though, as I was watching the spider shooting lighter than air filaments to support the new trap.

I reflected that the spider had not tried to recapture the freed ant, though it probably could have. There had been no pause for an "oh shit" or fit of pique. It just went back to work. Now it was singlemindedly engrossed in its task.

I wish I could concentrate like that, could focus so utterly on the desired goal. Most especially, I wish I could similarly know when to simply have the grace to let go--and get on with my life. But we humans tend to dwell on lost friendships, dead pets, mid-life crises, a parent passing away, a child's death. We need time to grieve what is gone or what might have been.

And that's OK. That's what makes us human.

Truth in the Blame Game

The trip to the vet's
Was routine today.
Vaccines delivered--nose nicely wet.
All's quite A-OK.

So if the dog's not sick,
What's that horrible smell?
Did trepidation of the doc
Make him gaseous and unwell?

'Tis a scent of great shame,
Out-stenching a hog.
Wish he could take the blame,
But that isn't the dog.

Astonishing Visitor

The day was already hot when I went out to water the garden one morning in late July and caught a glimpse of a bird munching the remaining raisins on the grapevines. I did manage to see a white wing bar on a black wing, a red face, and bright yellow underparts, but the vision was so brief. The specter saw me coming and scooted through the shade and leaves of the grapevine, slipping out through the holes in the fence. I burned the image of it into my memory so as to be able to look it up in my books later, after finishing my chore. In the meantime, I reluctantly settled for being mystified.

Later, when I sat with my books, I worked back and forth through the "could have been that" options until I finally found a picture of what I had seen--a western tanager, a male, the first time I had ever seen one.

The book said they are birds of the spruce and pine country. So what was it doing in the middle of the desert, in the summertime, stuffing itself on my raisins?

The western tanager was first identified on the Lewis and Clark expedition and recorded in their logbook. Lewis sighted it in Idaho, long before the uncharted territory was called Idaho, of course. It has been found inhabiting environs as high as 10,000 feet. It is most commonly found in the mountain country from Alaska down into the Rockies.

I can only guess that it was on its way to southern climes for the winter, but July seems an early start on that trip. July is full-bore brain-cooking hot. It tricks humanity into believing summer will never end. Could migrating birds already be planning on winter? Or perhaps I'm famous for my raisins amongst the tanager community?

Whatever--I'm just glad that I got the opportunity to see one without taking myself up to the pines to do so.

The bird was kind enough to make the trip instead.

Now my official policy is to leave a few raisins on the vine every year. This surprise visitor is welcome back.

(Since the time I wrote this, I've discovered that the tanager I saw was, indeed, migrating. Breeding season is triggered in birds by the lengthening days of spring. After the Summer Solstice, the longest day of the year, June 21st, the days grow shorter and avian gonads shrink into dormancy until the Winter Solstice, December 21st, after which the lengthening days will rekindle their urge to migrate and procreate. So late July, while still hot and summery by human standards, is post-Summer Solstice by a month. Well into the season for migrating, as far as birds are concerned.)

Unto Death

They made a unique pair.

Her family pioneered our region of desert, something she frequently pointed out to the rest of us "God-damned pilgrims" on a regular basis. That was our moniker on a good day. It was often worse.

Her grandfather ran cattle over the land now governed by our homeowners' association--long before barbed wire fences divided the land--before electricity--back when windmills pumped the only water for fifty miles in any direction. She grew up thinking of all the land as hers, though only a small portion of the acreage grazed was actually owned by her family. She worked it, loved it, and lost most of it in a bitter divorce settlement that left her with little. Ten acres, a rock and mortar house with dirt floors, a few pigs, several horses, a few head of cattle, and a windmill running dry. That was it.

I admired her fortitude. She rose up from her ruins to go back to school to become a nurse. She bought a small townhouse in the city near her school and job, where she lived with her six-year-old son. Her sixteen-year-old daughter stayed at the ranch with a hired hand. Those years were tough, but she was tougher. She looked "rode hard and put up wet" as a friend put it, but she hung on. She was a survivor.

How she hated it when her windmill ran bone dry. That meant she had to come to us "pilgrims" to get water. She negotiated a deal through one of the developers of our section of land, since she refused to deal with our Board of Directors. Legally, she could not get water from us without becoming a member of our association. She got her water, but insists to this day that she did not join the homeowners' association to do so. Association lawyers determined in a later deposition that she was a member, but she said no. I saw her as flexible. She was a member when she wanted to be. When her new husband served two years on the Board of Directors, she was a member. When it came to paying her water bill...maybe she was, maybe she wasn't. When it came to annual assessments--she wasn't.

I was Secretary and Treasurer of our fledgling homeowners' association. It was my happy duty to deal with her when she mostly wasn't a member of our association. I had to bill her, press her to pay and endure her threats when she did finally pay. Dealing with her was an exercise in human psychology. I dubbed her "Pioneer Woman," PW for short, because I knew she saw herself as being the rightful owner of the land. The rest of us would always be interlopers in her eyes.

Keeping pigs was forbidden in the CC&R's governing our association, but nobody wanted to confront her over hers or explore the issue of grandfathering pigs in. She threatened to shoot anyone who drove by her property, saying that the road by her place was privately owned and off-limits to the rest of us. But she was flexible again in that it was OK by her if we maintained her road. She developed a feud with a young mother who she claimed drove by her too quickly when she was out on horseback, spooking her horse. When the mother stopped to discuss the matter with her, PW wound up shrieking curses. Another time she reported the same driver to the police for spooking her horse into throwing her. The mother claimed PW had been walking the horse when she drove past, not riding at all. The investigating officer decided PW was jealous of the mother because she was so much better off financially. The mother just thought PW hated her because she was there. She called PW "the neighbor from hell."

PW did remarry. He too was a survivor. She met him in the hospital. He was one of her patients. He had some Vietnam related injuries. (She was a great nurse, by all reports. One neighbor who came across her there and was under her care said she was professional and caring.) Her new husband wore scruffy, baggy jeans and shirts and a shapeless hat. His hair and beard were gray and untrimmed, flowing to his shoulders and down his chest. He spoke with a slow drawl and was never hurried. This was a good thing, as his battered pickup was at least ten years beyond hurrying. He shared PW's opinions of the rest of us. He too had grown up in rural Arizona and saw us as idiots when it came to ranching and knowing the land. He was right, of course. We didn't know much. We were escapees from suburbia. He was clearly enamored of PW, though, so I dubbed him "Devoted." They made a good pair.

About this time, one of our association members came down with cancer. He lived alone with his wife, a victim of MS. She was spunky and served on the Board for a term, but she had severe physical disabilities and she could hardly care for herself, much less him. I told her about hospice. Several of us said, "Call if you need help." She never did. Toward the end of a miserably hot July, he died.

Afterwards I had her over for dinner several times before she moved away. She told me how Devoted and PW had often come to their assistance during her husband's illness. When he fell and was too weak to get up, she called Devoted and he came to the rescue. A number of times Devoted delivered dinner to them--his specialty--homemade pea soup with ham. Ham from the pigs he wasn't supposed to have, pigs he slaughtered and smoked himself. He made it a habit to come by on trash day, pulling the city bin to the road and back for them. When the sick man's invalid wife couldn't change the bandage over his oozing tumor because of the stench, PW stopped by daily to do it. The dying man and his wife relied on their assistance. They became good friends. Faithful unto death.

Hearing her story, I was amazed. Such compassion from folks the rest of us often found threatening and confrontational! They were providing help while the rest of us were just offering.

They're unique, alright. PW and Devoted are that in spades. Unique expressions of human complexities--for better and for worse.

Flowing Uphill

Alarming, whirling, burst into flight,
Rising up like a swell on the ocean,
White-winged doves' sleepy roost disturbed.
Dawn's walker incited this commotion:
Communal peace momentarily deterred.

Airborne stampede, frantic wings whistling
Dart down, swoop left; one-minded in flight.
Mountain sings now of rest and good will.
Flock hears, adjusts, and quickly tacks right.
Gray wave answers by flowing uphill.

How different the quails' sound,
Like hail on tin roof--their noisy eviction.
Exploding on high into fear's frenzied flight,
Constantly calling their loudest conviction,
That safety requires their formation be tight.

Legion, the silver torsos with top-knotted noggins,
One in their searching--sanctuary the goal.
Mountain's refuge, available still.
Singularly willed is their aggregate soul.
Gray cloud answers by flowing uphill.

Dragonfly Midwifery

The Hassayampa River is an "upside down river" for most of its course from its headwaters in the Prescott region to its termination in the the Gila River, south of Buckeye. By this I mean that its flow is primarily underground. There is a stretch of river a few miles south of Wickenburg, however, where the solid rock of the terrain forces the flow to the surface, creating a riparian oasis currently owned by the Nature Conservancy, an organization dedicated to preserving natural habitat and biodiversity.

Part of the preserve is open to the public. Trails wind around a natural spring and pond, through mesquite bosques, shady cottonwood/willow forests, and alongside the river. The visitor's center is an adobe building, once a ranch and stagecoach stop for those traveling from Phoenix to Prescott. The huge palm trees that flank the offices were imported by early American pioneers from Castle Hotsprings, Az, where they are indigenous.

A few miles south of Nature Conservancy headquarters there's a Rest Area on the west side of the highway. In the past this spot was a campground and 'poor man's swimming pool." Trucks with campers or trailers would stay in the parking area overnight, sometimes longer. Especially on the weekends, families would picnic on the grounds and play in the river. Now fences close off access to the river; no one is allowed to spend the night, but the toilets and picnic area are still well used. Nature Conservancy has managed to protect the river here and allow it to heal. That's the gain. The loss is that now there is no wading, dam building, tadpole catching; no mud fights, soggy clothes, ruined shoes or sand tracked into cars returning to town.

During one visit I made in the days prior to The Conservancy's guardianship, I waded upriver in a flow that barely covered my feet. While the river can be mighty in flood, it is normally not much more than a trickle, but in Arizona--where water is gold--that counts as a river. I was watching for tiny fish, floating seeds, bugs or crawdads, whatever might float my way and snag my attention.

All at once I spotted one seriously ugly waterbug. I don't count most bugs as cute, but this one was something I felt sure its own mother wouldn't claim. I had no idea what it was, but its repulsiveness was downright fascinating, so I paused to watch it's tumbling course in the river's current.

As I stood by in attendance, it crawled from the water onto the damp sand of a small bar. I watched as its exoskeleton split open along its back. Then buds formed on its dorsal surface which ever so slowly unfolded as the creature pumped them full of fluid and sunshine to become crystalline wings. I gazed in amazement at a process as old as time, the birth of a flying antiquity. For 45 minutes I stared, spellbound, at the metamorphosis of a waterbug into a skybug.

As the wings slowly straightened and strengthened, the dragonfly tested them, quivering them against its new element. When the wings were deemed flight-worthy, there was one final buzzing pre-flight, then it was gone in the blink of an eye.

I've gone to the river many times since then and seen lots of ugly bugs, but never again have I had that rare privilege of dragonfly midwifery. Now that the river is supposed to be off-limits, I wonder how many will ever share that experience with me.

Part of me rejoices at the sight of trails leading from the fence to the river, proving that others besides myself still duck through the obstruction and make the pilgrimage now and then. Probably the same part of me that delighted to see the verdin drinking. A part that refuses to be defined by expert's definitions, diagnoses or fences.

Perhaps dragonfly midwifery is alive and well, despite the fence.

Antelope Squirrel Hanging

Sometimes we don't get to know the "hows" and "whys" of life. Sometimes there is no answer. It just is what it is.

One day I came upon a teddy bear cholla in which a dove was impaled, wings spread as if in flight, like an airplane making a really horrible landing, hitting the runway moments before the landing gear unfolds. It was frozen in death, an ice statue in the summer heat. Perhaps a sudden gust of wind, a dust devil maybe, had thrown it into the cactus as it struggled for control of the air currents. Possibly something spooked it from its roost and in panic it flew into the spines which held it, like a bug on a board, until it died. There is no "why" that matters now, not to the dove. Life? Death? It just is what it is.

Another time I found an antelope squirrel hanging by the scruff of its neck on the quill of a staghorn cholla, not a mark on its body. Did some predator hang it there? Meat on a hook, a meal for a later time? Did the squirrel slip as it stepped gingerly onto the quills in search of a spot to gnaw past stickers to the green skinned flesh of the cactus--sometimes all that's left to eat at the end of a desert summer bake-off? The "hows" don't matter anymore. Not to the squirrel. It just is what it is.

The dance of life and death....

An old man told me of the time on Lake Mary Road when he suddenly felt compelled to pull off the pavement, stop, and enjoy the summer day. A deer abruptly darted out of the woods, bounding across the road in front of him, a cougar inches behind. The deer made it back into the woods on the other side, but not much farther, he figured. The cougar had been too close. A magic moment, a gift for him alone to witness--an opportunity to glimpse the awesome, brutal miracle of the dance.

And awesome it is.

A neighbor told me how her cockatiel escaped through a door one of the kids had left open a moment too long. As it flew to a nearby tree, a Cooper's hawk hit it mid-air. "My pet died in an instant," she said. "But it was the most beautiful thing I've ever seen."

In such spellbinding moments, we are laid open to the mystery, the one we know we can't control or choreograph. We are waylaid by surprise, by the dance.

Are these sorts of moments prevalent in the climb up the ladder of success? The rush to the store, the after-school sporting events, the grocery store? No, the busy-ness of life makes the dance harder to see--difficult to remember.

A most unfortunate forgetting.

Still...whether we remember to remember or not--it is what it is.

Water in the Desert

On my way down the hall I glanced out the window at the two-inch high circular water dish in the courtyard. A fat toad was lounging in it, every evidence of bliss shining from its amphibian face. Golden eyes were half-closed, and was that the ghost of a smile on its yellow lips? Its bulk took up nearly all the space in the dish, displacing the refill I gave it not two minutes ago.

Nevertheless, there was enough space between the toad and the edge of the dish for the lapping of one jackrabbit tongue, the owner of which crouched and watched me as it continued to slake its thirst, content it had nothing to fear so long as I stayed in the house. The rabbit held its position; the toad was obviously not going anywhere. I paused to savor the scene.

To quote C. S. Lewis, I was "surprised by joy." Surprised by a moment that united the three of us in awareness shared.

Natural Cures

Typically I applaud efforts to use natural cures. I prefer a holistic approach to healthcare as opposed to the array of specialists who subdivide their clients, focusing on the parts relevant to their own expertise, frequently failing to consult with one another, though they all strive to heal the same patient.

I tend to choose herbs over pharmaceuticals, though I don't deny that the latter have their place in the scheme of healthcare and are, from time to time, the best choice. I don't see modern Western medicine as the opposite of traditional, indigenous therapies of Eastern or Western origin. I believe they can be compatible. But I do lean toward things more natural, less invasive, lower in side effects--whenever possible. Sometimes, though, natural cures are just plain hideous.

Newspapers are delivered about 4:00, before the summer sun has risen and blasted any semblance of cool from the ethers. The woman who delivers them must have struck it as she made her rounds. There just isn't any other traffic at that hour.

An hour after her delivery, the dogs and I were passing a neighbor's house that stands quite isolated from other residences. Their garbage can stood next to the roadside, ready for pick-up later in the day.

Next to the bin lay a jackrabbit, injured in its hindquarters so severely it could not run, but not so severely as to kill it outright. No injury showed on the surface of its body, but internally--perhaps the pelvis or hips were broken. The fore part of its body was whole and the rabbit was completely alert. I had only a glimpse of it before it began to struggle to flee, which attracted the dogs' attention and swift response.

The youngest went in for the kill. The injured jack fought valiantly for its life, screaming in fear, fury and pain. My attempts to call off the dogs were futile, and after two endless minutes, the terrified squeals stopped. It was more than I could bear to witness. I left for home before it was over, hands over my ears, tears streaming down my face.

The dogs followed later, carrying their prize into the driveway. I put the jack's carcass in my trash bin--ready for pick-up later in the day.

I know the dogs were doing what came natural to them. I know the jackrabbit could not have survived. I know it would have died slowly in pain and shock in the desert's mounting temperatures. The dogs delivered a much swifter finish. I know all that. But this natural cure is....

In <u>Earth Prayers From Around the World</u>, May Sarton writes:

Kali, be with us.
Violence, destruction, receive our homage.
Help us to bring darkness into the light,
To lift out the pain, the anger,
Where it can be seen for what it is---
The balance-wheel for our vulnerable, aching love.
Within the act of creation,
Crude power that forges a balance
Between hate and love.

Help us to be the always hopeful
Gardeners of the spirit
Who know that without darkness
Nothing comes to birth
As without light
Nothing flowers.

Bear the roots in mind,
You, the dark one, Kali,
Awesome power.

Runoff

T he only consistency is inconsistency. One of life's inconsistencies results from runoff. Flash flooding is full of surprises, not all of them pleasant. That's a consistency. Nevertheless, rushing waters do tend to bring people together, either to watch in awe and wonder, to give assistance, or both. Every desert dweller has runoff stories. Here are some of mine.

An example of how selective storms can be: recently, after a sudden summer downpour that lasted only 15 minutes, I discovered the washes around my house were running quite respectably--meaning there was enough flow that I couldn't jump over it, but not enough to prevent my walking through to get to the other side. I figured the large wash a quarter mile east of me would be really dramatic, so I hiked over to inspect it.

As I walked, I noticed the ground became dry. It didn't appear a single drop had fallen here, though my house had been drenched. The wash I sought was bone dry!

The washes around my house were obviously part of a different drainage system than the large wash to the east of me. The day's cloudburst was evidently so localized that just one of the two drainage systems picked up any flow. I find that pretty amazing.

Another story involves the time I tried to cross a wash in my truck after watching some teenage boys wade across on their way home from the school bus stop. They lived just north of my house, residents of a foster home in which troubled teens were housed by the state with a couple of adults dedicated to getting them through high school and providing the parenting they lacked. An enormous challenge, featuring lots of parent-teacher conferences, counseling and fist fights between their boys and others, including my son. I saw the water had come up to the guys' knees, but thought I could still make it.

I did--halfway.

When the truck stalled, the boys came back into the rushing waters to push the truck up the opposite bank. Their kindness surprised me.

When I tried to start the truck, it wouldn't.

Another neighbor witnessed my difficulties and decided to park and wait for the waters to recede before attempting a crossing. She let me use her phone to call the local garage, about five miles away. Homer answered. That was amazing in itself because Homer lived his vocation like a hobby. You never really knew when he'd be open, but if you waited long enough--he would be. Another surprising thing about Homer was that he never blew himself up. With his habit of chain smoking inches away from the engine he was working on, constantly leaking ashes onto his patient, both of them covered in oil and other flammables, I always expected to hear he'd met his end explosively, but he died of a heart attack instead. The cigs did get him, but not as I expected.

Anyway, he was still very much alive at the time he picked up the phone in answer to my distress call. He told me to just wait, that I'd probably splashed enough water onto vital parts that it couldn't start up just yet, but would when it had the chance to dry out. As a mechanic, Homer preferred the old-style cars. If computer chips were involved, he wasn't, so I wasn't usually a customer unless I needed a battery, or something very simple. His advice, though, was right on. I spent the next half hour chatting with the neighbor who owned the phone. Afterwards, the truck started up just fine. I'd scared the crap out of myself, but found some reliable friends.

And then there was the time I was driving home, following a neighbor in a small pickup he'd just bought a week before. There was a Nissan truck on the road in front of him. The wash just this side of his house was a major one--had a name on the map and everything. It was running high. The Nissan went right through. He figured he could too.

But the waters had eroded away the streambed and it was deeper than it looked in some spots--not the ones the Nissan had traversed--only the ones Guy, my neighbor, chose. The engine stalled with the cab in the water, but the bed on high ground. He wasn't going to wash away, but the cab was getting pretty dampish. His sense of priorities kicked in. Maybe he couldn't save the new truck just yet, but he was damned if he'd lose his Tony Lama boots. He stripped them off and tossed them into the bed of the truck and waved me off, telling me to try another route to my own house. He was going to wade across to get home and wait for the waters to drop. Home was only a couple of hundred yards away--through waters rushing with prickery shrubbery of all sorts, waiting to puncture tender bootless feet--but God save the Tony Lamas.

Another neighbor was a bit more luckless when she got caught in her old sedan in a wash during a runoff. Her car started to meander downstream. She had her two small children with her, but they all got out and across to the opposite bank. About a half mile from home, she squelched water with each step in walking there. (She wasn't wearing Tony Lama's.) She called her husband and he came to tow the car out when the waters died down. With the help of a blow drier and the summer's heat, they dried the vehicle out. It ran just fine, but ever after, it harbored a horrible odor. Large purchases of pine tree car deodorizers couldn't touch that overpowering aroma. Old and reliable as the vehicle was, it had to go.

Ahhh, runoff. One of life's consistent inconsistencies.

Enthusiasm Reborn

Every Sunday I go to church. Nature is my church. I hike into a local canyon, not for endurance, but for peace. It's my time and I'm possessive about it. I go at or before sunrise to escape the heat and other hikers. I want the place to myself.

I go about a mile up the gorge to a well-shaded rock. There I park myself with binoculars, water and a field guide to birds. Then I wait.

My time has often been rewarded with sightings of coyotes, javelinas, deer, rock and antelope squirrels, and many varieties of birds, bugs and reptiles. I've even heard bobcats yowling to one another high up in the canyon walls.

Petroglyphs cover the rocks the whole length of the trail, showing the significance of this spot to ancient peoples for many centuries--Hohokam, Yavapai, and the unnamed wanderers that came before them.

Because I'm in a county park, I know I'll have to share my space with other hikers. They usually aren't many in number, and don't remain long, finishing the trail and turning to hike out after a brief greeting to me. The early hour deters crowds, leaving me stretches of time for self-renewal.

One morning, however, the scene was anything but meditative. I was the first one out to my rock, but I was closely shadowed by a couple who turned around immediately and hiked out. As they left, another couple arrived, then families, then teenagers exploring together, then a man and woman with a picnic basket. The place was Grand Central Station with not a shred of peace or quiet. No coyotes, no deer, no squirrels--even the birds were silenced by the constant flow of human conversation. I waited for the flow to ebb, but they just kept coming. I felt frustrated. Eventually, though my rock was still shaded and would be for another thirty minutes, guaranteeing me a comfortable perch, I packed up my things and left. I was disgusted and discouraged to have my plans for the morning thwarted.

As I started back down the trail, I saw a red-tailed hawk sail into the canyon. It alighted in the canyon's rim for a minute, watching the people traversing the floor. That gave me plenty of time to inspect the bird through my binoculars, the first opportunity I'd had all morning to see any wildlife. When it took flight again, it circled and sailed above us, screaming all the while. I was amazed it was so boldly calling attention to itself. It put on quite an aerial display. As far as I could tell, I was the only person to notice.

There are times you know you've been blessed, given a treasure beyond words, a greeting from the cosmos. I had my personal affirmation, one I could only acknowledge with awe and humility--and enthusiasm reborn.

Of Stealth and Neighbors

Sex: marital, premarital, geriatric, pedophilic, incestuous, kinky, illicit, celibate, sadistic, masochistic, homosexual; whatever the form and style preference, it's part of us all. Every society has its sexual taboos. Because every culture needs to. No segment of any culture is untouched by sexual urges that test its taboos. No subset of society is immune, be it presidents or priests, scout leaders or scholars, doctors or docents. Is there some guaranteed healthy method to balance sexual and other life urges? Some sort of wisdom minus rigid absolutes?

He was eleven when I moved into my house. He lived in a trailer with his family, my nearest neighbors. He had an older sister, and attractive, friendly parents who worked outside the home. Both were deeply religious and in later years became ministers and missionaries. When they moved away, it was to live closer to a congregation in the city that regularly financed their missionary trips into foreign countries. They were serious about doing good and saving others.

Out of boredom, he often came over to visit and play with my son, who was much younger. There just wasn't a companion any closer, in age or location.

As a new homeowner, I was busy planting trees and bushes. I was outside a lot, and he soon learned what a source of entertainment I could be. I've always talked aloud to myself, whatever I'm doing. He learned he could sneak up on me, hiding behind mesquite or creosote, and get an earful. If I spotted him, he'd dash away, laughing. I remembered playing similar games with siblings when we were young. As a countermeasure, I learned to watch my dogs, who no longer barked because he was a familiar, but they would still perk up their ears and stare off into the desert when they heard him approach, giving me a clue that more than the desert might be listening.

One time he told me he wanted to be a Green Beret. I wryly told him he was learning the stealth he'd need in that job by sneaking up on me. He shyly hee-heed. He stopped visiting to play with my son as older kids moved to our area.

Several years later another family moved into our part of the desert. They built a barn where they lived amongst stacks of furniture, animal feed, tools and boxes. Riotous clutter. They had power, but no air conditioning or heating. It wasn't all that pleasant indoors and there wasn't much to do, so their teenaged son found his own entertainment.

Her son liked to walk around the neighborhood, his mother said. He always knew who lived where, who had the new pickup truck, where new homes were going up. He met and made friends with my eavesdropping neighbor. Together they began peeping into the privacy of their neighbors' lives.

I suspected who was outside the night a camera flashed outside my bedroom window as I lay in bed, watching TV, but I had no proof. By the time I got outside, no one was there. I didn't report it to the police or the parents, not wanting to implicate when I couldn't be sure of the culprits.

A year later, a house was built north of me. The woman who moved there reported that one night she'd heard a noise and went out front, expecting to see some wild animal foraging in the darkness. Instead, when she turned on the exterior lights, she saw two bodies lying face down in the yard. In her shock and panic, she thought they might be dead, or at least injured, so she ran back inside to get her husband. Naturally, by the time the couple got back, the "bodies" were gone, but she remembered what they had been wearing.

The next day she saw two teenagers, dressed as she remembered and knew they were the two looking in her windows the night before. She brought the issue to their parents. One boy was the Green Beret hopeful and the other was the kid from the barn.

As far as I know, the voyeurism ended. The family in the barn eventually moved and my stealth neighbor grew up, got a job, and lived at his parents' place with a young woman and her two kids. That relationship didn't last, though.

The next incident occurred with another woman neighbor. One day she came over to ask me what I knew of the guy across the street. It seems he had walked out of his parents' trailer and over to her as she groomed her horse, stopping fifty feet away to just stare at her. He was completely naked, clothes in hand. He didn't say anything. Neither did she. He just stared until she walked away, went in the house and called the police.

The kid that loved to sneak up on me had taken his activities up a notch. He was continuing to pursue his sexual gratification down avenues that would only lead to more and more trouble.

Balance? He was no more headed in that direction than the Green Berets.

He moved out; I don't know where. His parents left our area a few years later. I hope he found the help he needed. His parents' religion wasn't his answer, but maybe he found some other one. I hope he found wisdom somewhere--found how to redirect his sexuality somehow. Found the compassion necessary, both within and outside himself, to initiate change.

Sex--part of us all, and part of the redemption of us all.

Of the Senses

Five senses, have we, through which we sample life. My dictionary claims a sixth. It calls that one "balance." Balance is what ties the other five together, avoiding extremes of likes and dislikes.

Sight: Framed in Navajo White

Only the very heights of the thunderheads reflect the pinks and bronzed-gold of the already set sun, contrasting with the broad, flattened black/blue water mist of their bases. Their billows rest, ominous with stormy promise, in the midnight blue of a pre-star sky.

The gentle southern hills have not lost their covering of creosote and palo verde to the obliterating descent of approaching twilight. In the arms of valley folds, deep in shadow, the lone house's windows show no lights. The city, in the lower, larger valley, also has yet to reach for artificial day, the birthing of those lights moments away.

Finches and sparrows come to roost for evening's rest in the nearby bush. They perch, dance skittishly, perch again, until the precise spot is found for the day's final blessing--sacred sleep.

Horned owl forsakes the recesses of his ancient, mistletoe-burdened palo verde tree. He slips into a low glide over the desert's floor, eyeing grasshoppers jumping below, sailing on silent wings to settle on the tip of a dusk-shadowed saguaro to survey the sands for movement.

The moon, nearly full, already risen, shows the crystal clarity of its blue basins, marring the ghostly white of the light shed in competition with sun's vanishing rays. Day exhaling, night inhaling.

The scene sanctifies me, the observer, watching from the window recessed in a wall of Navajo White.

Sound: Wind Voices

Pausing to listen, I hear the swelling power of one-voiced distal wind before it shatters into many-voiced proximal wind by...

Rattling in the leaves of the eucalyptus, a sound that ebbs and flows like the tide, leaves clashing, branches creaking where they rub together.

Shaking the dried seed pods on the palo verde as if a million tiny rattlesnakes awoke to danger at the same moment.

Whispering through browned, long-dead grasses, spent of seed, now just tinder for the next spark.

Moaning in the place where cliff wall has a hole worn after years of wind's efforts, a window no bigger than a peep hole, but enough to create a whistle that modulates with the force of the wind.

Whipping sand from the road and casting it to pepper against the lava-pocked terrain, with a sound like hard rain or fine hail.

Screaming as it passes through the multiple limbs of the century-and-a-half old saguaro, rocking the giant while the cactus slices its force into minutia of sound with needles that efficiently protect green-ribbed flesh.

A symphony for any who pause.

Smell

As I recall the spicy aroma of catsclaw
In thin catkins of yellow flower
In the cool of a spring morning,

The syrupy sweet aroma
Of the mesquite blooms
Alive with insects,

The scent
Of wet dust, rushing
On the wind that brings a storm,

The smell
Of hot creosote
In the blistering afternoon heat,

The pungent odor
Of a gently pinched leaf

Of Indian tobacco

The musky stink of wet bird waste
On rain-soaked soil
Under roosting trees

The stench of Chia's unique
Layered
Blooms

The burnt-wet rot
Of lightning struck
Dying saguaro

I become it.

Touch

As I hike I feel:
The wind flowing through the pores of my hat, drying the
sweat on my scalp.
The sticky, glistening resin on creosote leaves.
The tugging of the map in my hands, trying to race away with
the wind.
The burn of sun on skin on my calves, already blotching red.
The scratch of drying Fiddleneck against bare legs.
The biting of flies and gnats, the curse of the waterhole.

The coolness of a stream soaking my boots, disproving the claim of waterproofing.
The weight of my backpack, slung between my shoulders.
The reprieve of a cliff's shade, during a break for water and food.
The down-puffed broom seeds, windblown across my cheek.
The sting of sand in a dust devil's embrace.
A butterfly's shadow landing on my hat's.

Taste

The peppery-sweet aloe bloom,
The bitter creosote tea,
The filling malva leaves,
The fresh grass shoots of spring,

The bounty of saguaro fruit,
Mesquite-cured peccary jerky,
Gift of a hunter's kill,
The ephedra high of Mormon tea,

All offspring of earth and sky.
As am I.

Balance: Equilibrium

I read a Buddhist teacher's explanation of the Tibetan Book of the Dead. He said it was the story of the psyche's journey after death, blazing a path between two extremes. The soul of the recently dead must confront different manifestations of states of being, and choose its path while experiencing attraction and repulsion for the pair of opposites immediately before it. This realm of choosing is called the Bardo. The object is to pass all the pairs of opposites by the middle way, and thus find freedom.

It seems to me that the Bardo doesn't just begin with death.

Life is the Bardo too.

Orphanhood

He was headed home and I was on my way out, when we passed on the road that afternoon. When he saw me, he slowed and rolled down the driver's window.

Though he lived just west of me, and we had done each other numerous good turns over the years, we chatted only occasionally. I'd heard him screaming at his wife, periodically, in the heat of domestic dispute. Other neighbors even called the cops once. Because of his volatility, I chose not to become real chummy. Still, as neighbors we'd had dealings, lended a hand when needed, talked when we were both working in our yards or walking the dogs, waved as we passed each other in our vehicles. This time, though, he wanted a word.

"Well, I'm an orphan," he declared.

I already knew that his mother had died in a car wreck when he was nine, so this must mean his father was now dead too.

"My dad died over the weekend," he continued. "I'm not going back to the funeral because I can't take the time off work. Besides, I was with him a month ago. We knew this was happening, so I spent some time with him then. I got to see him when he was still alive. No sense going back now.

Still--even though I knew it was coming, I feel strange. I'm an orphan now."

I expressed my condolences, we both went our ways and my mind started working on that "orphan" thing.

My mental image of an orphan entailed a child, around age ten, tattered clothing, scrounging for handouts, you know--sort of Oliver Twistish. Now here was a thirty-three-year-old man telling me he was an orphan.

I guess we all have that child within that feels just a little more secure having parents around as backup. The loss of that relationship, at whatever chronological age, makes that inner kid feel the world's a tad bit more fearsome, that he's a little bit homeless, a bit emptier of comfort and a little more aware of his own mortality.

Orphanhood, I guess, has no age prerequisites.

Hitchhiking Spider

While spiders are certainly one of God's creatures, they are also one of God's creatures I least prefer to find on my person. I'm aware of their value in the scheme of things, helping to keep other insect populations in check, serving as food for birds and lizards--I don't doubt their value in the life cycle. I even get a kick out of coming across a tarantula now and then. I had one in the garage once and just left the door open for when it tired of exploring and decided to leave. I like spiders, so long as they're outside and not on me.

Once, though, I drove by the mailbox on my way out to do some grocery shopping. I pulled a large stack of mail into my lap. There was no traffic except me on our local dirt road, so I quickly sorted through the mail while slowly creeping along at five miles per hour.

Suddenly, a huge wolf spider shot out of the stack of mail and raced across my legs. I lost track of its progress after that, due to hysteria. While flinging the mail across the truck and squirming around in my seat to see where my companion had gone, the truck continued to slowly roll down the road, over the dirt berm, finally stopping when it hit a saguaro on my neighbor's property.

She was outside at the time, watering some trees and watching the whole scene in amazement. Very concerned, she kindly approached and asked after my health. She didn't even laugh when I told her what had happened, something I'm sure I couldn't have accomplished. She just looked at the green chunk missing from her cactus, the dent in my fender, and said, "I keep telling my husband we should remove that cactus. It's just too close to the road," as if the saguaro was to blame for the accident.

The fender was warped, but the truck quite drivable, so I went home and called the insurance company. The agent couldn't refrain from snickering a bit, but admitted she too had trouble remaining calm while wearing a spider.

Once again I attempted a trip to the grocery store. I was mindful, believe me, of the fact that I did not know where the wolf spider had gone, preparing myself for a sudden visitation at any moment, which I was determined would not result in any further accidents.

Was it under the dash? Under my seat? Crawling up my leg? Happily, it did not put in an appearance. When I parked, it was in the full sun. I left the windows up and hoped that a full hour of furnace-like summertime heat would bake any life-forms present. It worked. The next time I vacuumed the truck, I found the spider dead, in the door pocket under my maps.

I have a friend who used to deliver rural mail. When I told her my story, she assured me that spiders very frequently inhabit mailboxes. Next time I should just calmly take the mail, edge it under the spider in my lap, and scoop it out the window.

Obviously an experienced scooper herself, I could only sit in awe. This put a whole new face on that "Neither rain nor snow..." Mailman's Motto. I gained a deeper respect for the profession. Fortunately, for me, there has never been a "next time." I still warily check the box for God's creatures each time I remove my mail.

Autumn

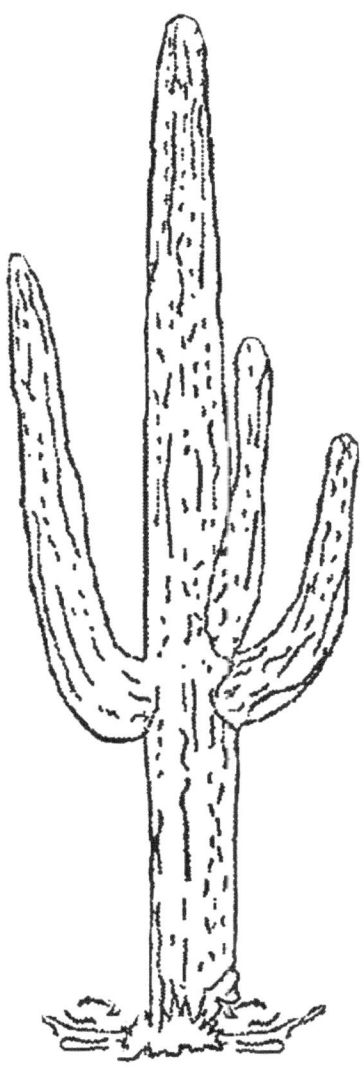

Miracle in Grass

The oriental concept of Yin and Yang is symbolized by the circle, half black, half white. In the white half a black spot sits; in the black half, a white spot. Neither half is pure; both contain elements of the other. This image represents life, which in its singularity is the circle, but which is experienced as pairs of opposites. Together, the wholeness of one creation. As pairs, they are white/black, male/female, day/night, life/death: the opposites, simultaneously whole and half, as life is simultaneously temporal and eternal.

* * * * *

This is no minor miracle!

It is, after all, September, end of a relatively rainless summer. There are no annuals left, having dried and crisped long ago in the summer's heat. The grasses of spring are dead, still standing only in places they grow thickest--under trees. These vestiges of the once green are protected by the tree's branches from at least part of each day's scorching sun and the trampling of animals, which would otherwise break the brittle stalks for scattering on the next breeze.

Yet here, in the guardianship of nothing more than a foot-high triangle bursage, is a clump of big galleta, a native grass of the Sonoran desert, victorious at the end of the killing season. It clings to the banks of a small stream bed, cut alongside the dusty road. The bursage beside it is dried and apparently dead, awaiting the next rain's reviving waters. Everything around the grass witnesses to summer's devastation, but it remains green. I have no explanation.

Is it the white spot in the black half of the circle?

And where's the black spot in the white half of the circle? For death is ever present in the midst of life. There is no place free of it, only seasons where it is more easily forgotten.

In most parts of the country, that's the summer. Winter is the killing season; winter is what thins the ranks of what nature has called into being, both flora and fauna. Summer is what grants the illusion of endless abundance and eternal life.

In the desert, though, summer is the killing season. Spring is abundance. Lasting only a couple of short months, spring is a bursting of life in underground burrows, in nests, in the greening and flowering of plants, all quickly decided by the presence or absence of rain.

Grasses sprout with winter storms and are matured and seeding by April, for May will bring the first round of the heat that will turn the world of annuals and many perennials into dead, brown, brittle lifelessness. Often in less than a week, the fragility of the annuals has proven their undoing for another year. With the comings and goings of the rains, the desert continually reminds that life and death dance together in making up the circle of life.

It was the dogs, actually, that pointed out the big galleta to me. They stopped to munch its green leaves for the chlorophyll so lacking in their diets. I was fifty yards down the road before I realized they weren't with me and went back to investigate. Then I saw the resilient stand of grass.

The next day, one of the dogs went into a desert broom bush and began munching again, revealing another clump of big galleta. More green in the midst of the season's brown. Another spot of yang light in the sea of yin black. Miracle times two.

Even in the heart of death, there is life. Rebirth is ever just around the corner.

Update 4

The heat of the desert summer has been broken. It is mid-September and the mornings are noticeably cooler. The night temperatures are dropping below 80 degrees, though not by much. The rabbits, birds, lizards and squirrels are spending their days someplace besides the shade of my patio and courtyard, proving existence no longer depends on staying away from direct sunlight.

Those born in spring and summer have been tested by the dryness and heat. Those who passed the test, those who survived, are now young adults who will breed next spring. For now, we all heave a sigh of relief. Summer is spent!

Nevertheless, the new quail family that comes round still has youngsters small enough that they must have been late starters, a brood of mid-summer, perhaps. They come in each morning, watching to see whether the dogs and I are sitting outside and whether we appear to be at all interested in their approach, so they can make a quick getaway, if need be. There are two adults and six chicks, just drifting into their adult plumage. Their topknots are ridiculously scrawny, but at least they're present, as opposed to when they were younger. With a little more time, they will become at least as charming as their parents'.

For all the numbers who did not survive the summer, who became fodder for roadrunners and snakes, there are these that made it. They will see to it there are more chicks next year, and all the years to come, so long as we humans allow them the habitat they need for life.

So much of the desert around me is being plowed under, scraped clean of any and all native life, in favor of the tract homes that preserve not a shred of the rich environment that thrived before them. This concept of beauty I cannot understand.

I grew up in a neighborhood that had also been scraped clean. When we first moved into the house, a large tract of land nearby was still desert, its native self. I always preferred that to my backyard. We kids knew it was destined to be a park, but we loved it just as it was. My brother rescued loggerhead shrike chicks from some boys intent on destroying their nest and raised them on waterlogged dog food until they could be released. I loved watching the life cycle of the frogs and toads that appeared magically in the "lake" after a rain's runoff filled a depression in the terrain. California poppies carpeted the desert each spring and we played tag with tumbleweeds rolling in the winds of autumn, even though being "tagged" meant pulling out stickers that made us itch.

Eventually, the park was finished. Now my parents' house is next to acres of grass and shade trees, tennis courts and Little League fields, a haven for joggers, dog walkers and nightly drug transactions. That, I am told again and again, is progress.

At the edge of the park, where it has been landscaped with desert shrubs, mesquite and palo verde, the quail families still have a small foothold in suburbia, still scuttle their broods from yard to yard to feed in constant conversation and communal comment. For most of their former, native neighbors, however, there is not foothold enough.

Encounters With A
Western Screech Owl

I was charmed at first sight.

I saw something fly from a low spot near a palo verde tree to the mesquite nearby. Just a flash of gray. At first I thought "dove" but there was something not quite dovish about the way it darted through the palo verde, hugging the cover of the branches. Perching in the mesquite, it turned to face me. Glowing yellow eyes calmly returned my wondering gaze.

I was being blessed with the gift of a close up encounter with a Western Screech Owl. Great Horned Owls, Barn Owls, once a glimpse of a Burrowing Owl--these I'd seen before in my neighborhood, but that dusk, just about the time it was rousing for a night's activities, I had my first encounter with a Western Screech.

I got plenty of time to stare at that fabulous face through my binoculars. It did eventually bolt when I made a move to walk past, again flying below the canopy of surrounding scrub, but not before giving me great looks.

The Western Screech is mostly gray, marked with black mottling. The shoulder blade feathers are white tipped and form a white V-shape on the back. It's a small owl, only about seven to eleven inches in height and weighing in at about four ounces. The bill is black, with a cream-colored tip. It sports ear-tufts, but on this occasion, they weren't raised.

A week later I approached the same place from the opposite direction and spotted my wild neighbor sitting on the ground at the base of the palo verde tree. It froze, allowing me to walk past without spooking. This time the ear-tufts were up like symbols of alarm--or at least extreme caution. Part of its camouflage involved watching me through eyes narrowed to slits, aware, no doubt, that its wide-open, bright yellow eyes would have announced its presence like headlights on a rainy day.

Immobile as the tree stump it stood beside, I wondered if it would turn its head to watch me go by. It did exactly that, keeping its face toward me as I moved along, with that owlesque fluidity of neck muscles that appears to be no motion at all. I laughed to watch it. I couldn't have been five feet away.

I've been by that spot a number of times since then, but have not seen the Screech. No matter. I've already had two treasured sightings, and these I remember when I hear its "bouncing ball-like" call at dusk or dawn.

My last birthday present from a friend was a Western Screech Owl nesting box. It's ensconced in a palo verde just east of the house. Maybe I'll have more encounters with a Western Screech.

Cardinals and Sandpipers

Cardinals mate for life. They also hang out together all year long, not just during the breeding season. They will counter-sing with one another, one starting a phrase and the other finishing it. The male brings the female snacks during courtship, a ritual indulged in before each nesting. There might be four broods a season, but two is more typical. While the female builds the nest alone and incubates the eggs alone, the male feeds her on the nest, and when the eggs hatch they both work to exhaustion caring for the young.

Sandpipers are polygamous, both sexes. They mate frequently and with as many partners as possible. They propagate and nest inland, tending the chicks for barely two weeks, often abandoning them before they can actually fly. The adults then leave to migrate to southern climes. The young fend for themselves until they mature enough to become airborne and follow.

Some humans are cardinals, some are sandpipers.

The birds are lightyears ahead of us though, for it would never occur to a cardinal to try to convince a sandpiper to become a cardinal. Nor would a sandpiper try to convert a cardinal to sandpiper sexual practices. They know their own kind immediately and never waste a moment of time or energy on the other species.

If only we humans could differentiate so readily!

Strange Bedfellows

One morning's walk, I found a spot in the road where a mouse and a scorpion had both been run over. They were side by side, almost touching; the scorpion flattened like a pancake, the mouse squashed on its side, guts spilling from its belly, brains from its crushed skull.

If they died together, which is how it looks, what forces put this twosome in the same place at the same time? Hunger? Curiosity? Dumb luck?

None of the participants in the moment can give me a clue now.

It's a mystery.

Cat Collage

My neighbor broke his back in a construction accident and for months was confined to a body cast and special hospital bed in the living room of his trailer.

I stopped by to visit one day after work and he told me he had that day watched helplessly through the screen door as a coyote crept up the pine stairs to his door and snatched his cat off the porch where it had been napping in the morning sun.

I didn't know what to say.

* * * * *

I used to have cats.

When I discovered I was allergic to them, I stopped replacing them as they disappeared. They were all spoiled, loving house cats that left each night to explore and prowl. Eventually, they didn't return.

Yes, it might have been owls. Great Horned and Barn varieties might have taken them. Cats, after all, are smaller than a good-sized jackrabbit, and owls take them.

One time, though, I walked out front of the house in the early evening and saw a coyote crouching, shielded by bursage, right by the path my cats and dogs used to head south on their nightly hunting rounds. There, I suspect, was the solution to the missing cat mysteries. This hunter had figured out the nightly pattern of prowling. It was only a matter of time before its stealth paid off.

* * * * *

There's a sign at the corner. Someone is looking for their big, black and white Manx. They offer a reward. "If you find it, please call...."

When I mention the sign to my neighbor, I ask whether she's seen it too.

"You know, they're never gonna find that cat," she says.

She used to have cats too.

Some Snake Tales

Everyone who has lived in the desert has rattlesnake tales. Some have rattlesnake tails, though that sort of collection has never appealed to me.

The first of my tales occurred when my son was five. He got a new two-wheeler BMX bike for his birthday, very cool and blue in color. He wasn't really ready for it, though. His coordination wasn't good enough, but after months of wishful thinking and aborted efforts, he decided it was time to give it his best shot.

I was enlisted to run alongside the bike, providing the support and balance needed to get the rider in the groove. Training wheels were really not an option due to our dirt roads and gravel driveway. It was also a matter of pride. Training wheels were for babies and he was no baby.

Most afternoons we could be found outside, practicing. At first, I couldn't let go of the bike at all without causing a mishap, but as my son improved, he managed to pedal a couple hundred feet unattended and began leaving me behind in the dust.

Steering was still uncertain, but stopping was a major challenge. Actually, stopping wasn't a challenge, but stopping gracefully was. He progressed through a "slow to topple" stage of stopping that had numerous hazards, but was hysterical to watch. It was while he was at this skill level that we had a snake encounter.

A neighbor boy of eleven often came by to witness our training sessions and give advice from his older and wiser perspective. He and I were both running alongside at the start of this particular trip, but eventually my son went wobbling off on his own, leaving the two of us behind. He slowed to the point where wobbling and steering competed with disastrous results, strayed off the path, up over the berm, and fell sideways into roadside thistles and thorns.

The neighbor boy and I tried--really valiantly--not to laugh, but I'm afraid we were as we trotted over to render assistance. My son was still under the bike, crying and complaining loudly about the stickers in his hands, but mostly just mad we were laughing. At him, not with him. As the friend lifted the bike off my son, I grabbed his arms to help him stand. We were chuckling as we helped brush off stickers.

Then we saw it. Our hearts stopped as we saw a coiled Diamondback rattlesnake blinking in the sun, still stunned from our biker's fall onto it, sure something had just happened to disturb its nap, but unclear just what. We backed away quickly, gasping in shock.

"You fell on that snake. Oh shit!" the neighbor exploded.

"No I didn't. I fell next to it," my son disagreed, as if that made all the difference.

"You fell on it. I picked you up off of it," I insisted.

"Did not."

"Did too."

"Oh shit."

"Did not."

"Did too."

"Oh shit."

While my son and I argued the whole walk home, leading the wayward bike by the handlebars, our friend could do nothing but repeat, "Oh shit," shake his head in wonder, staring with eyes wide with amazement.

The snake, I presume, crawled home with a headache.

* * * * *

The next tale involves my two dogs--one that never did grasp what was happening, and the other, who grasped not only the situation, but the snake too.

A warm, early fall twilight was descending as I left the house with my dogs for a last minute walk. Poor lighting prevented our being able to see the rattlesnake stretched across our path and my shepherd-chow mix and I nearly stepped on it.

In an instant, the night's stillness erupted with noise and activity. The snake, startled out of its blissful snooze, rattled, coiled hastily, and began striking repeatedly. It struck air frantically and blindly, unable to pinpoint the specific danger.

I pranced backwards, trying to remain airborne as long as possible to avoid the fangs. My Chow-mix was oblivious. He watched me in amazement, confused by my odd behavior, unaware of the snake striking between his legs. My Australian Shepherd raced into the fray, snatched the snake up in his mouth and tossed it into the bushes alongside the driveway, barking to keep it at bay while I dashed into the house for the shotgun I used to dispatch the poor, confused, but still dangerously disturbed reptile.

I can't believe one of us wasn't bitten. And who would have suspected such bravery from my clownish Australian Shepherd? Not I.

My hero got an extra portion of dinner that night.

A Gift of November

I remember one birding outing with Maricopa Audubon from Phoenix. We spotted a small hawk perched in a tree some distance away. Scopes came out to augment binoculars and a discussion ensued as to whether the bird was a Cooper's or Sharp-shinned. Both hawks are accipiters. They are medium sized, long tailed, short-winged and not prone to soaring. Their flight consists of numerous, quick wing flaps, then gliding--quick wing flaps, then gliding. They are so similar in appearance that even experts can have difficulty telling them apart when perched. And I'm no expert. As the debate continued, I busied myself watching an osprey settle on a telephone pole to rip apart the fish just plucked from a lake. Better to wait for those more knowledgeable than myself to figure out the hawk question. They never did, though. We moved on down the trail in the firm conviction that the perched bird in the distance was either a Sharpy or a Cooper's.

Occasionally, though, events conspire in such a way that divinity stands readily apparent and proximal. The encounter feels calculated. Chance plays no role.

As I walked my usual path on a cold November day's pre-dawning, a soft whistling diverted my attention because I could not remember having heard it before. Crossing a dry wash, I glanced downstream at the silhouette of a dead tree containing an accipiter. I never would have seen it at all if it hadn't called to me. It continued its quiet mewing, though it knew I was there because I answered its conversational intonations. I stayed still, for I could feel its nervousness. Nevertheless, it remained for another minute, then excreted, ruffled its feathers and jumped into flight beyond my line of vision.

I was astonished by its boldness. I knew it for a raptor by the shape of its head, an accipiter by the length of its tail, but I'd never been so close to one before. I knew it had consciously called my attention to itself. We had shared a moment of Biblical "knowing" of one another. Not sexually, of course, but in awareness of oneness; we were connected.

Later in the walk, after the sun had risen, the bird sat in attendance once again. It flew over my head to land in another dead tree ahead of me, fully in the open and clearly watching me. It was much more comfortable with my presence this time, and sat as I marched right below it and paused to see its markings. Then I left. But was it Coopers or Sharpy?

Once home, I checked my books and realized the bird had provided me with all the clues I would need. According to The Raptors of Arizona, I had visitation with the Sharp-shinned, "a secretive hawk of the forest," wintering in the desert, which "seldom perches in conspicuous locations." The book continued, "even experienced ornithologists sometimes confuse" it with the Cooper's unless "vocalizations are heard," for then they may be readily distinguished. "The common calls of the Sharp-shinned are a repetitive mellow *kew kew*." The Cooper's calls are harsher and raspier. "Vocalizations are not often heard outside the breeding season or far away from the nest, however."

I heard its gentle mewing in November, hardly the breeding season. It gave me the gift of broken patterns of habit so that I might know it--so that I might "know" it.

And in that "knowing" I learned not only its identity. I felt our interrelatedness, our mutual sacredness.

Divinity, residing in the soul of a generous hawk, reminded me of my own.

Sonoran Snow

The Desert Broom
In full fall bloom
Buzzes with myriad bee voices.

Erect, evergreen branches
Brooms for men's ranches
First in pioneer and indian choices.

Native toothache cure:
Chew a stem, cleaned and pure,
A pain-relieved patient rejoices.

Female plant's white flowers
Fill December's chilly hours
With snowy, silky, airborne seed.

Wafting off on every breeze
Each child's playtime to please
When jiggled branches fill entertainment's need.

Drifting, airy, snow-like billow
Gathering at base of desert willow
Responding to life's germination creed...

More Brooms, more Sonoran Snow.

Winter

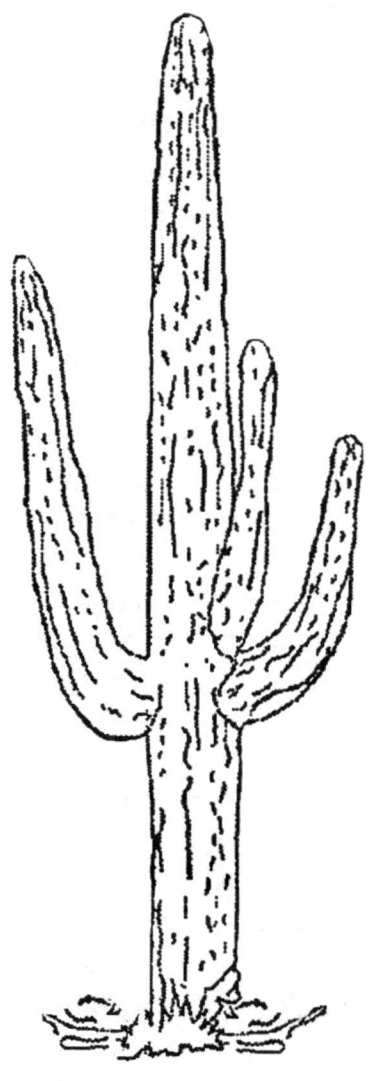

Merlin Magic

There are times when the bird feeder has not been emptied by the close of day. This never happens unless there's been a new face in amongst the daily regulars. A face that isn't interested in seed and causes the sparrows, finches, doves, quails, cardinals, towhees, thrashers etc. to hang back in the creosote, hiding. When this happens in the winter, I begin looking for merlins.

I first saw one when I noticed nobody was scarfing up the seed I'd just scattered, rare behavior indeed for the piggish birds that feed in my yard. I went out to hunt for the hunter and glimpsed a small raptor shooting from a creosote patch, flying low to the ground, expertly keeping the moderate canopy between itself and my line of vision. It was small and dark. That's about all I could see. That and the fact that it could fly like the devil and the sparrows were rightly afraid.

Later I saw a pair sitting companionably together on the garden fence. Male and female. So different that I never would have guessed them to be the same species. Merlins demonstrate incredible sexual dimorphism. The male is smaller than the female, nine inches long to her twelve, and bluish in dorsal plumage. Females are brown. These falcons breed up north, but winter throughout Arizona. Males are only slightly larger than the kestrel, but they are heavier on the wing and don't hover as kestrels do. They are powerful hunters, adding a new element of terror to the lives of the seed-eating bunch. They easily live up to their moniker, "Pigeon Hawk," though they prefer smaller birds. When I saw my visitors together on the fence, they'd just finished gulping down a dove, as evidenced by the pile of gray feathers beneath them. Even so, no small birds were moving around the feeder, just in case the predators might want dessert. When the merlins saw me, they exploded into flight, dropping immediately to skim the desert floor under cover of the foliage, fleet stealth so typical of their species.

My vision of these handsome hunters was brief, but impressive. I'm sure the sparrows would beg to differ, but I hope merlins are always winter visitors to my yard.

Two Frequent Fliers

First there's the cactus wren. Being a bird, flight is natural, so of course he's a frequent flier. The largest of the wrens, the cactus wren is Arizona's state bird. Their bright white eye stripe is distinctive. Their rusty brown backs and tails are barred with black. The breast is white with black spots that often coalesce into a black breastplate. The lower bellies are a warm, peachy color. Even more distinctive, as far as I'm concerned, is their personality.

Bold, brassy and brazen, these clowns are the first to explore the inside of your car when you leave the window down. Open garage doors are invitations to satisfy their curiosity about what's on the shelves, in the box, or behind the freezer. Nevertheless, they do exercise some caution. They are ready to flee at the first sign their wanderlust is becoming dangerous. Join them in the garage, and they're gone.

Bold enough to nest at eye level in the cholla ten feet from the house, the parents shush the babies squealing to be fed when I walk by. They perch nonchalantly with bugs in their beaks, pretending their only intent is to pose with their prize, waiting for my exit to dash to the nest and feed their young. They apparently believe their subterfuge has kept me from spotting the nest or knowing what they're up to.

They are the only birds audacious enough to join me and the dog as we sit on the patio breakfasting. They love eating the dog biscuit crumbs left behind and approach me closely to obtain those delights. One morning, as I sat writing, a wren waddled toward the crumbs. I sat perfectly still in order to see just how close it would dare to come. Intent on prowling, it was fully aware of each breath I took, but unconcerned so long as I made no move. I didn't block its path to the repast, but it hopped onto my foot, where it remained for ten to twenty seconds. From there it cocked its head, looked into my face from around the notebook I was holding, waited until it saw it had my attention, then hopped down to make quick work of its feast. It didn't *have* to perch on my foot. It chose to.

I was delighted by the prankster's trust.

Another frequent flier in my neighborhood is one for whom flight is not natural. He has to have an ultra-light to accomplish the feat. Recently endowed with a pilot's license, he offered a ride to a friend and myself. We leaped at the chance.

Unfortunately, it was July when he made the offer. Two could fit on his ultra-light, so he could take one passenger at a time, but we'd all have to lose lots of weight if we hoped to get aloft in the summer. We agreed to wait until winter.

A cool, clear morning with sixty miles visibility and little to no wind -- the day chosen for our flights. A brown wall of smog was settled over Phoenix, but points north and west of us were spared. Conditions were perfect for our purposes.

I got the first ride. I was strapped in and shown how to use the communication system so we could talk to each other in flight, provided we yelled loud enough to be heard over the engine. The pilot, a big guy, took his place, in front of me. It was a tight squeeze on the open frame of the plane, with me practically straddling the pilot, but once we gained altitude and I felt the cold blast of air above ground level, I was grateful he blocked some of the wind and his body heat kept me a little warmer.

We flew along the Central Arizona Project (CAP) canal. He pointed out my house. Then we headed north to where he had carved a small landing strip out of the desert by driving his Bronco back and forth over a stretch of level ground and pulling out bushes and cactus in the way. We were high enough to see the green, rolling hills around Lake Pleasant and the empty Hassayampa riverbed. Dirt roads were everywhere, like arteries across the landscape. I was amazed by the sheer number. We looked for wild burros, but spotted none. The pilot indicated how green it was north of the canal, proving that the natural flow of water across the terrain had been affected by the CAP, however much the engineers tried to prevent it.

To the south, the White Tank Mountains loomed. Westward we could see small rural communities and the landing strip, where jets from Luke AFB practice "touch and goes." Farther off was Vulture Peak near Wickenburg. It was amazing to be flying, feeling the wind and the slippage of the plane through the air currents, so intimate compared to airliners.

I wasn't scared at all and wore a huge grin the whole ride.

It ended all too soon with a flawless landing. When I congratulated the pilot with a "Hey, great landing" as we taxied, I heard him saying the same thing to me. It was a little disturbing to note we *both* sounded amazed.

Reluctantly, I gave my place to my friend so she could have her ride. I assured her she'd love it. As they zipped by me on the runway, gaining speed for takeoff, I tried to capture them in a photo. I was close enough to see the huge grin on her face.

May both these neighborhood frequent fliers see many more years of sky time.

Cosmic Fireflies

A treasured memory of my childhood is my parents rousting us out of bed to watch fantastic lightning displays as storms swirled around the valley where Tucson is anchored. Angry clouds and wind turned back on themselves by mountain ranges kept us in suspense. Nature's wild-willed revelation was not to be missed, whether or not there was work or school the next day. We stood before the picture window in the den and marveled. Special effects in the movie and TV industry were in their infancy, so we were still astoundable. Lightning spider-webbing across the night sky and thunder bouncing between heaven and earth amazed us.

One in the morning, and I'm up for another sort of natural lighting display. In heavy robe and winter slippers, I'm bleary-eyed and shivery on the rooftop--waiting. Warned about the meteor shower tonight, I'm chilling from my feet to my hair, which is still damp from having been washed earlier.

I want to witness the night sky's disquiet, but first I silently observe the impaired peace of the desert around me. Somewhere a mourning dove is startled into flight for some unseen reason. A great horned owl hoots its four-noted phrase and is answered by another at a distance. Something calls with an odd barking sound I can't attach to any known species. Horses rumble in the corral next door. The palo verde tree, a black, macabre silhouette against the lighter soil rustles with the movement of something large and heavy in its limbs, but that creature remains unrevealed. The night is restless.

Then, in the east, the sky takes up the agitation. Flashes of light appear. Some are quick bursts, short-lived in the atmosphere of Earth, but others make long streaks, darting from horizon to horizon like embers escaping from a hidden campfire. They aren't terribly numerous. About one every minute. For all the fear and consternation they caused in olden days, in the minds of more primitive people, it's not all that exciting by modern standards. Today's high tech kids have their virtual reality games to offer a fast paced alternative to the comparative dullness of a meteorite shower. Probably too tame to warrant getting kids out of bed for--especially on a school night.

When the fiery skyrockets slow in frequency, I turn to go back inside. My hand on the door knob, another noise carries across the darkness to my ear. A father's voice calling his daughter in from the display to return to bed.

Perhaps techno-play hasn't spawned immunity to natural wonders, at least not in everyone. Some still watch cosmic fireflies flashing above. Some still leave their dreams to witness Earth's.

Coyote Commentary

This morning as we trekked the road winding around the base of the mountain, the dogs' attention was suddenly diverted to something near the western foothills and they gave chase. Although the sun had already cleared the horizon--just barely, I couldn't see the cause of their enthusiasm, but figured it must be close.

Not far from here, on a previous dawn, the dogs took off in hot pursuit of a coyote they'd seen in a wash west of the mountain, demonstrating the same sort of commitment they were showing this morning. They have their priorities. Rabbits startled near at hand elicit a prompt and immediate response of canine joy in the chase. The territorial challenge of another dog brings on a rush of urinating and furious scratching to reclaim the region as their own, but coyotes... Coyotes are my dogs' bane.

I'm sure as far as the wild dogs are concerned, it's mine that are the trespassers. Coyotes know they are the rightful, though furtive, possessors of the land. Being omnivorous, they creep into my yard and eat whatever leavings I've put out for the birds and small beasts. If they scare up a rabbit on the way, so much the better. They stealthily drink from the water bucket as soon as I've brought my dogs in for the night. When curiosity, or perhaps audacity, holds sway, they peek in the arcadia door to see if my pals are lounging in the living room. If they are, and remain undisturbed, the coyotes may pilfer unchallenged. If they rouse the dogs with their reconnoitering, they know to move on until things quiet down on our homefront. They mark bushes, defecate in spots sure to be noticed by my pets, scratch the earth and rub against creosote in timeless rites of ownership and dominance.

Naturally, my dogs are most offended by these calling cards, an open challenge to their authority. Domesticated they may be--in part (at least they sometimes play that role for my sake)--they ache to prove their capacity to defend their turf. After such flagrant flaunting of their doghood, they are required to give chase, hot with fury, at the slightest glimpse of their wild cousin. It matters little whether the intruder is actually invading their personal real estate or not.

This particular morning, I continued walking when the dogs rocketed off in passionate pursuit of their traditional mockers, expecting them to catch up to me again shortly. Much later, though, when they hadn't returned, I called and whistled. Silence was my answer.

I considered worrying, but had heard no reason why I should--no sounds of fighting--so I continued on my way. Eventually they rejoined me, tongues hanging down to their paws, exhausted, but unharmed. At that moment a wailing from the top of the mountain took up a sarcastic soliloquy.

I looked up to see a coyote calling from the ragged, rocky ridge, clearly commenting on my dogs' returning to me--probably some canine version of, "Yeah, run back to Momma,"--tamed away, as they were, from the wild. The younger of my two couldn't pass up the defiance from above and started back up the mountain. The coyote, though contemptuous, had no intention of making good on his ridicule, and turned to flee his sanctuary.

A call to my dog and, more likely (if truth be told) the coyote's disappearance, stopped his climb and we resumed our morning's walk. His safety ensured, the coyote returned to his station on the ridge.

From there he heckled us, unable to leave well enough alone. From his summit's perspective, he could witness every step of our journey, clear back to my yard, a distance of a couple miles. For the next half hour he announced his insults to highest heaven every move we made. He was joined by two others of his clan, but they remained silent, leaving the taunting to him. He told it like it is, who the real masters of the land are, and the real dogs too.

"Hear ye, hear ye: we fled only to avoid having to shame you pathetic excuses of dogness in battle, something we could easily have done. Never doubt who's the real King of the Mountain!"

Clouds Sleeping Against Earth

Winter's morning haze,
Thickest before sunrise,
Conceals every aspect of Phoenix
Except the mountaintop standing close,
Peeking above the billowing vapors of
Clouds sleeping against Earth.

Ground-bound spirits gently swirl,
Depositing a droplet epidermis to:
The leaves of black-barked bosques of mesquite,
The spider webs marking flights of passage,
The curling hairs of my head and hand,
Etched now in glistening dewy diamonds.

The full moon setting behind moisture's wall
Shows a body white with reflected light,
Ringed by empty darkness,
Layered again with a band of gold,
Rounded distally by a coppery skin.
Night's globe races Daystar to opposite horizons.

Rising sun wakes winter fog,
Stirring clouds from sleeping posture.
Water droplets outline every leaf.
Fog's gray shadow shattered by
Heliocentric rays darting to become
The cardinal perched in palo verde tree.

One Winter Day

The pre-Christmas day dawned cold and sunny. Clouds overhead dotted the sky like sailboats in a summer regatta, but not so thick as to prevent the sun's rays from reaching earth. The north, however, promised a storm that flexed its water-blackened cloud muscles, perhaps over Wickenburg, or maybe Yarnell.

I was headed in that direction, having set aside another Sunday morning for self-renewal at the Hassayampa River Preserve, located just south of Wickenburg on Highway 60. I hoped I could get in a few minutes with the river environs before the storm struck.

I was granted an hour. Through winter coat, gloves and two layers of socks, a bitter breeze worked to freeze fingers and toes. My nose was numb and running. My fingers worked stiffly to focus biroculars on the few kinglets that flittered in the nearby trees The leaves of the winter-thinned willows and cottonwoods rocked at anchor, ready to follow those that had already given way to the temperatures and wind, carpeting the forest floor and pathway to the lake.

Ducks hurried past me, as they floated by my position on the shoreline, insecure until they put me behind them. They flowed information across the glassy surface of the lake. The coots and moorhens, though, barely noticed me, continuing to graze on water plants. They had their priorities. My presence didn't divert them.

Three sora, small rails that seldom fly, called to one another from the reeds through which they waded, laughing as if insane.

Then, with a quiet whoosh I first took to be the the wind's voice, the rain began pitting the lake's face with fine droplets that turned almost immediately to sleet. The tiny beads of ice convinced me to be on my way, but before I reached the car, it was snowing.

Desert dwellers are pretty much snow deprived, usually by choice, so when it snows, it is big news! As I drove into Wickenburg, the Phoenix radio station I listened to was announcing that snow was falling in Carefree and Cave Creek, and, in fact, all over the north valley area. I wondered if it was falling at my home in Surprise.

I stopped at the restaurant where I often breakfasted on Sunday mornings a little earlier than usual since the weather had forced me to leave the preserve sooner than was my custom. It was packed with folks, every one of whom seemed to be staring out the window, watching me park. I couldn't imagine what I was doing that was so fascinating until I realized they were staring at the front of my car, coated thickly with snow. They could see snow falling to the ground, but it wasn't yet sticking there. My car, though, was another matter and they were amazed by the coating of big, fat flakes on the grill.

Evidently they wanted only to watch it fall, not go out into it, because I waited for a table in vain. I bought a newspaper and left for a nearby Mexican restaurant I figured would be less busy. It was, and I had my omelet and coffee there with an assorted clientele that had been at the car show in the city park next door until the snow convinced them to find warmer quarters. A couple from Colorado sat at the table across from me.

"We left home to get away from this!" he repeated, over and over.

Those of us from Arizona's desertlands, though, just kept looking out the window, big grins on our faces. I wondered if my son was seeing this at home.

After breakfast, I went to visit a friend who lived near the hospital. Driving down her street, I passed three look-alike brothers, bundled against the cold, ungloved hands red from pressing together wet snow to form paltry snowballs. There simply was not enough of the stuff to do a snowball justice, but they were trying. As I drove by, I expected to be pelted, and they probably wanted to, but they waved instead. They reminded me that desert kids will never miss those rare opportunities to play in a snowstorm. We didn't. That will never change from one generation to the next.

I remember those snows in Tucson. What a joy they were. We knew the first snow was also likely the last of the season. Later, in college in Flagstaff, a northern, mountain town, the freshmen could always be spotted because they got up in the middle of the night with the first snowfall. Upper classmen knew there would be plenty more where that came from and stayed in bed.

Sitting in my friend's living room, we each sipped a cup of tea, well removed from the cold. We watched with delight as the flakes fell huge and thick--thinned to smaller--then got huge again. They coated the cypress trees in her yard, bending the branches under heavy, white blankets. Creosote bushes sagged under their load, sheltering quail beneath, who peeked out at their unrecognizable surroundings. Mesquite branches, sporting similar snowy burdens, seemed to drape icicles in the wind, but a second look proved them to be old, dried seed pods. The gray sky undulated. It constantly shattered into flakes that fell to earth, whitening as they descended. Inside, we applauded the scenic splendor, contrasting so nicely with our warm tea.

Hours later, I drove home through a desert where snow remained only in those spots most protected from the sun, which was making short work of the storm's effects. At my house, there was no sign of snow, though everything was wet.

My son was not home, but I found his note on the kitchen counter:

"Mom--it snowed here. My girlfriend, the dogs and I all played in it. Hope you got to see it too!"

I had.

Cold

The coldest cold you'll ever meet,
One truly that you'll ne'er fergit...
A winter's morning toilet seat's
Far colder than a witch's tit.

Cold hands and even colder feet
Upon a lover's sleeping form
Guarantee that he will greet
The moment with a moody storm.

What mother hasn't gravely cautioned
Her kids from the bottom of her soul
To never take part in crazy actions
Like licking a winter-cold flag pole.

Not even the bare-handed feel
Of ice-coated pailed water
Whose surface you find you must peel
To slake thirst's nasty slaughter,

Matches the shock and torpor
Beyond all comprehension or compare,
Of stumbling in a sleepy stupor

Gooseflesh erecting each body hair...

To visit that early morning abode
The place where bodies and minds are relieved,
The throne, the "head," ever blessed commode,
That arctic perch that leaves butts so grieved.

For...

The coldest cold you'll ever meet
One truly that you'll ne'er fergit
A winter's morning toilet seat's
Far colder than a witch's tit.

Christmas Lights

Some of my neighbors put up their Christmas lights just after Thanksgiving. I enjoy seeing their displays as I drive home after dark. I always chose not to put up lights because the eaves are on the second story of the house, too high to reach even with my extension ladder. Attaching lights to stucco didn't seem wise either, so I just didn't have any. This year, however, after being inspired by my neighbors' efforts, I decided to put lights on the front entryway, on the wrought iron in the arched windows and the front gate. Just strings of tiny, white lights, but they shout "holiday" and I don't know why I didn't do it years ago.

I leave the curtains open at night so as to see the lights whenever I wake up and be cheered. Later, when I have the tree up and decorated, I'll spend a couple nights on the sofa so I can feast my eyes on the tree's multi-colored lights whenever I turn over. I love staring at the tree a minute or two before drifting back to sleep. Actually, as a kid, I always wanted to sleep under the Christmas tree to enjoy the lights all night, but wasn't allowed. Now, as an adult, I make up for that holiday deprivation.

I leave the lights up through the twelve days of Christmas, perhaps a bit beyond, depending on when Epiphany falls during the week. Nothing comes down until after the Christmas Tree Burning Party, held the first weekend after the twelfth day of Christmas. I make a pot of chili and invite friends to bring their trees of Christmas past to the ritual tree burning in my yard. One year we had ten trees for the bonfire. Folks said they could see the fire for six miles. That was the year the fire truck roared out to my house from town. Fortunately, the firemen had a sense of humor. One I knew from the days our sons played soccer together, which also helped, I'm sure. The Christmas Tree Burning Party is the last fling of the holiday season and the first real occasion to blow New Year's dieting resolutions.

The day after the party, all the seasonal decorations come down. The first night after all the lights are packed away for another year always seems--so dark.

Winter Galleta

I tallied each clump of Big Galleta my dog browsed for chlorophyll earlier this year. None of the stands of grass he visited is showing the slightest green. They seem perfectly lifeless bunches of straw. Some seeds still cling to stalks, awaiting the next brisk wind or rain to dash them from their strongholds, but there is not a speck of verdure to be seen.

They made it through the heat of summer still carrying some color, but could not refuse winter's demand that they hibernate to rest and renew. I know their hearts still beat in the midst of the brown, fibrous remnants of leaves and that with the next rain and some slightly warmer nighttime temperatures, there will be a reawakening.

For now, what's left just rustles forlornly in the chilling breeze.

Christmas Bird Counts

In 1900 twenty-seven conservationists protested the traditional holiday hunt where teams competed to see who could shoot the most birds in one day. The conservationists decided to count the most birds they could in one day instead of shooting them, marking the start of annual Christmas Bird Counts, now a practice of lands as diverse as Alaska and Argentina, and of peoples from professional ornithologists to amateur hobbyists. With over 100 years of records from these bird counts, an enormous ornithological database has been formed to help determine the health of the environment and individual bird species. The decline or increase in species, geographical shifts in winter or breeding ranges and overall status of bird populations is documented statistically.

Example: the Bewick's wren is rarely seen east of the Mississippi. It used to be quite populous in that region, with a subspecies common in the Appalachian Mountains, but Christmas Bird Counts have long charted the changes that mark the Bewick's wren's demise in the east. They are not out of the ordinary in the west, though. The reasons for this change are not well understood. The Bewick's are known for their ability to co-exist with man, often nesting in old cars or abandoned buildings. Some experts think that competition from the more aggressive House wren accounts for the

Bewick's disappearance from the east, but the point is, records from 100 plus years of bird counts map the history of changes in this bird's populations. Identifying trends such as this cues in conservationists as to which species need special attention and assistance.

While the Bewick's has been declining, the Eurasian Collared-dove has been expanding its range. Originally from the Indian subcontinent, it began increasing its territory in the 1900's, reaching the British Isles by 1950. Today it can be found naturally as far north as the Arctic Circle in Scandinavia. It made it to the Bahamas in the 1970's with the help of man, and from there it began its conquest of the New World. In the 1980's it established colonies in Florida and began to spread unnoticed among the similar Ringed Turtle-dove population. By the mid-1980's, ornithologists caught on to the fact that they were witnessing the spread of a whole new species and started to pay attention. In this bird's case, the Christmas Bird Count data has charted the invasion and settlement of a new hemisphere.

My first involvement in a count was north of Wickenburg and included Arizona Upland Sonoran Desert Scrub habitat-- dominated by saguaros, ironwood trees, palo verde trees and mesquites, with bursage, creosote, brittlebush and assorted smaller cacti making up the lower canopy of ground cover. All day we walked dry washbeds, counting everything with wings. Each count region is a circle with a 15 mile diameter, so is large enough that only a sample can really be taken of the avian population residing there.

Every place we stopped we heard Verdins, often spotting them in their typical frenetic activity in the terminal ends of the branches of desert trees. There certainly seems to be no diminishing of their numbers, no immediate concern over their fate.

The second count I helped with found me in the desert near Arlington, Arizona. Here the desert is largely creosote intermixed with more creosote. We got our population sample by birding a small area, then driving to another, until we had checked five or six geographical areas representing our count circle.

Here too, I was impressed with the numbers of tiny Verdin we spotted. Their persistent, dynamic, mighty-midget presence was a consistent factor. They are here to stay, so long as we allow them habitat. May we always provide them that, for if we lose the Verdin, we are lost indeed. If we damage the environment so much as to prevent this little hardy soul's survival, we surely jeopardize our own.

By late afternoon energy wanes, and counting volunteers mingle at a dinner in which stories are swapped and numbers tabulated. It's a long day, made longer when the weather is inclement and if owls get counted too, for owling demands pre-sunrise or post-sunset efforts. But, the data gathered is valuable and friendships made are often renewed annually on favorite count sites.

A century of conservationist passion for birds and nature has its pluses.

New Year's Revelation

Another year gone....

My New Year's Eve is traditionally spent with a couple of good friends. I join them to watch rented movies and eat junk food, predominantly buffalo wings, until the countdown to the new year. That we toast in with a little wine, hugs and the appropriate ruckus of noisemakers. If we've timed things nicely, the movie wraps up just around midnight. Soon thereafter, I'm headed home to bed. It's dull by many people's standards, but suits me just fine. I can't imagine starting a new year without the company of these pals with whom I've shared so much life: problems with money, parenting, parties, beers, campfires, dinners, Sunday newspapers, and countless cups of tea and coffee. We've known each other for over thirty years and seen each other through many changes.

I always appreciate educational experiences too, so when one regarding aging gracelessly can be tied into a New Year's Eve celebration--all the better.

Last year my friends' neighbors were having a bonfire, burning their Christmas tree. They invited the son of my host over to party with their own kids. Later on, after midnight, when the neighbors called on the phone to wish us happy new year, the two men began talking. The neighbor told my host that he and the boys had had an impromptu contest to see who could pee the farthest across the fire. He lamented that he'd come up short, so to speak. Probably due to his age, he bewailed. I listened as my crony sympathized, saying he too had experienced some of the same signs of aging. He went on to say that lately, it seemed, increased effort to pee also increased the likelihood of pooping in his pants. Hearing this, I laughed so hard I nearly peed in mine-- the female version of a similar dilemma?

It's a good thing this aging business has its humorous aspects. Remembering those is a grand way to see in another new year.

Hummingbird Salutations

This winter I got to observe hummer behavior that was surprising because it was out of season. I have a Costa's hummer that owns my feeder. He patrols it and tries to keep other males away. He's there all year. Throughout the cold of winter, however, he was displaying ritual courtship behavior before a female as she sat in the open, the better to view his acrobatic exhibitionism. He rocketed high into the air over her, then dove in a half circle near her, finishing by shooting around high over her perch to dive again and again. She watched attentively. I can't say she encouraged him, except by remaining perched, but I don't claim to understand the machinations of hummingbird flirtation. Especially when it occurs outside of the normal mating season.

His unusually-timed passion was impressive. This Romeo was certainly intent on his Juliet. I hope I'll see the offspring of his efforts next March.

His trust in courting even when I was nearby, reminded me of one summer when I glanced out the window and noticed the shallow clay pot I keep filled with water in the courtyard had run dry. I went out to see to my duty of refilling it for birds, bunnies and whatnot. When I turned on the hose, I stood over the bowl, watching it fill with cascading fluid.

A hummingbird darted from its perch in a nearby oleander to join me. It hovered near the stream from the hose at the level of my ankles, drinking from the burbling waters before they hit the bowl. Clearly pleased with life, it then perched on the rim of the basin and preened in the splashes from the waterfall, occasionally lifting to linger over the liquid in the pottery, dipping feet and tummy in the bath before alighting once again to primp.

I watched, spellbound, seeing hummingbird hygiene up close. I marveled at its fearlessness, trusting me to provide cooling waters without harm. I carefully switched the focus of the hose to a potted plant. The hummingbird moved with me, floating on wing-thrummed air between leaves of verbena to drink again from the water's flow. Finally, its thirst slaked, it rose to the level of my face, stared me straight in the eye and very clearly indicated its "thanks" before buzzing off over the wall and out of sight.

Salutations to you too, little one.

Such summer memories can warm any winter day.

House Fire

Half the top story was already in flames when I left my house before dawn to walk the dogs. The gold-orange blaze lit up the western sky, shattering night's domination of the horizon. I couldn't be sure who's house was on fire, so I ran to the street for a better perspective. The tall Tudor-style a quarter mile away. I raced to the car, added the dogs, who were thoroughly confused at this interruption of their normal schedule, and raced down the road.

Running up the driveway, I saw a neighbor laden with an armful of items from the house. He said nobody was left inside. He was helping the owner rescue what they could. He thought it had started in the chimney. A teenager appeared, carrying women's clothing. He pitched it in the back of his pickup and hastened back in for another load. Hearing sirens approaching, I decided the best thing I could do was get out of the way. I drove back home and took the dogs for their outing.

While police and fire vehicles tended the inferno down the road, I ran with my dogs, too full of adrenaline to walk. Soon a helicopter hovered, filming for Channel 10, a clip that would make the noontime news and show flames shooting twice as high as the two-story home providing the fuel.

Exercise and breakfast over, I returned to the scene to offer condolences and see if there was anything I could do. The owners were friends of mine for over twenty years. I stood in the front yard with them, watching the ruination of years of dreaming, penny scrimping and backbreaking labor. Not to mention the innovative, one-of-a-kind decorative touches that only come with building your own home with your own hands. The lumber and brick they had salvaged from older buildings; the hardwood floors they'd installed themselves. It took them ten years to save for the staircase and railing they wanted. All gone. Lost in a morning.

Hummingbirds cavorted in the pine tree out front, oblivious to the destruction behind them.

The woman next-door brought over thermoses of coffee and water. I went home for muffins. Another took the owner's newly homeless dogs to stay in his pen until arrangements could be made for them. Several neighbors came to offer the burned out couple a place to stay until they were resettled.

A cardinal flashed by, checking out the commotion, rivaling the spent flames with his finery.

People showed up from the wife's work place. They'd bought clothes so there would be wardrobe options beyond what the family had on their backs. They also bought dog food for the pets, and sandwiches for lunch for those of us who stayed to start sifting through the ashes. Items the fire had spared were packed in donated newspaper, placed in donated boxes, stacked in borrowed trailers and hauled to a nearby relative's house. The response of family and friends was incredible.

"It could have been worse," the wife said. "At least it didn't happen while we had all our company at Christmas two weeks ago."

Hours later, exhausted physically and emotionally, those of us working salvage wrapped up and prepared to leave. I scanned the discouraging roofless brick facade left standing. The image of despair.

A verdin called busily from one of the trees in the wash nearby.

That verdin, the cardinal, the hummingbirds too-- reminders that life goes on, enduring even the darkest catastrophe.

We Should All Just Get Along

After his house burned down, my neighbor was astounded by the outpouring of sympathy and assistance offered by others. He was deeply touched.

The day after the fire, a small group of friends met to find salvageable personal items in the debris, pack them up and move them to safer quarters, all preparatory to being inventoried and cleaned by the insurance company. As we worked, a woman pulled up to the site in her truck and said she had a message from the president of our homeowner' association. Our lady president was getting lots of calls from people asking what they could do to help. Since she didn't know what the hapless landowners' immediate needs were: money, clothes, a place to stay--she didn't know how to answer. She asked the fire's victims to call her to let her know what she should tell those who wished to render aid.

Then the president's messenger went on to say that she'd been pretty self-involved lately. Her husband recently had surgery to remove a tumor and they didn't yet know if it was cancerous. She apologized to me for not contacting me over the Christmas holidays, something we normally did. I said the responsibility was mine too. She said she had a rum cake in her freezer destined for me.

After she'd gone, my burned-out neighbor mused about how often our own problems pale in comparison with other peoples'.

He remembered how long he'd been at war with the president of the homeowner's association. She'd accused him and his wife of misappropriation of association funds after he stepped down as president. The crimes of which he was accused were so ridiculous few considered her worth listening to, but in the absence of substance, she provided extraordinary quantity of rumors and was quite the thorn in his side. Now here she was asking how she should direct others to help.

"We should all just get along," he said to me. "Why can't we always be that generous and caring toward one another? Why must we fight? We should all just get along."

Later, as I reflected on his query, I remembered Ecclesiastes, chapter three.

For everything there is a season,
And a time for every matter under heaven:
A time to be born, and a time to die;
A time to plant, and a time to pluck up what is planted;
A time to kill, and a time to heal;
A time to break down, and a time to build up;
A time to weep, and a time to laugh;
A time to mourn, and a time to dance;
A time to cast away stones, and a time to gather stones together;
A time to embrace, and a time to refrain from embracing;
A time to seek, and a time to lose;

A time to keep and a time to cast away;
A time to rend, and a time to sew;
A time to keep silence, and a time to speak;
A time to love, and a time to hate;
A time for war, and a time for peace.

Why can't we all just get along? Because seasons change and that's not what human beings do in every season. The pairs of opposites are equally part and parcel of life. It's all about accepting life as it is, not as what we might wish it to be.

Still Life of an Eagle

A neighbor gave me an article about Aldo Leopold, a man who called himself an "ecologist" before the public had any idea what such a thing was. He was a scientist, a forester, a wildlife expert and a professor at the University of Wisconsin. He wrote books about the wilds of nature, which he loved deeply. That love taught the scientist's soul to sing.

His first job was in the forests of Arizona Territory in the early 1900's. The death of a grizzly bear in northeastern Arizona helped shape the philosophy behind another term he helped introduce to the English language, "biodiversity." A quote from his first book, <u>Game Management</u>, published in 1933, reads: "...twenty centuries of 'progress' have brought the average citizen a vote, a national anthem, a Ford, a bank account, and a high opinion of himself, but not the capacity to live in high density without befouling and denuding his environment, nor a conviction that such capacity, rather than such density, is the true test of whether he is civilized."

* * * * *

On a leisurely trip from Prescott to Surprise, a change in altitude from 5,300 feet above sea level to 1178, I paused often to enjoy the constantly changing scenery and environments.

The first stop was in the forest along Highway 89, just south of Prescott in the ponderosa pines. I hiked to a windy ridge paralleling the highway. A storm front was arriving from California to accompany me on my journey south--a cold, wintery one, at that. My hike was chilly, with few birds putting in an appearance save for a female downy woodpecker. On my way back to my car, however, I passed a small meadow where I had a ringside seat to the squabbling of a family of acorn woodpeckers and a glimpse of junco haven. Every kind of junco, a sparrow-like bird, scratched and pecked in the dirt by my car without regard to the traffic passing on the road nearby. I hiked a mile to see one bird, returned to the car to find twenty-five. Go figure.

Farther downhill I stopped to see a stand of mullein, an herb originating in Asia, transplanted here via Europe. It's not well suited to living in the desert of my home, so it's a pleasant find in higher climes, bringing back many memories of steamy cups of mullein tea from campgrounds in my past. I counted dead flower stalks from last year's blooming plants. Nearby new life sprouted from the seed they had sown. Biennials, it would not be until next year that these youngsters sent up a flower stalk to procreate.

In Yarnell I stopped at St. Joseph's Shrine, a cherished spot for birding and musing. I noticed the trees were budding, promising spring on such a blustery day! In the cafe on the edge of town I got a piece of apple pie. I asked a waitress about the signs I'd seen saying, "Stop the Mine." She said a Canadian mining company wanted to work the hill south of town. Some of the townsfolk were in favor of it. It would bring new jobs and money to Yarnell. Others were opposed. They said it'd be detrimental to the wildlife in the area, what resided year round and what migrated through. Yarnell, she said, had once been a bird sanctuary. While she leaned toward preserving the landscape, she had sons who wanted to be able to live and work in Yarnell, supporting their families in the manner to which they had become accustomed living elsewhere. It would be nice if they could move back.

There's the dilemma. Yarnell is just one of many places it's being played out.

Leaving Yarnell, I started down the narrow switchbacks that weave down the mountain to the town of Congress. Now the wind was blowing fiercely, buffeting the cliff face with dust and debris. Two golden eagles taunted the fury of the air currents. Only their incredible skill kept them from being dashed into the rocks. One crooked back his wings as if to dive, no more than fifty feet from my car. In the crazy winds, this allowed him to hover over me. He hung there, in the raging torrent, absolutely still, staring from me to the terrain stretching to the horizon, as if inviting me to share his eagle's perspective. I pulled off the road, not easily accomplished on that narrow stretch, in order to watch my still life of an eagle, utterly mesmerized.

He was so close I could see the pale sunlight glistening golden off the feathers of his head and neck. I could see the quivering muscles work to lock his wings in position so he remained hovering before me, not cast against the weathered wall of stone beside me, only ten feet away from him. His partner dipped and soared farther away from the cliff, exuberantly dancing on air.

Later, in swapping golden eagle stories with another bird enthusiast, I learned he had once seen an eagle sitting next to a badger hole. When the occupant left, the raptor snagged the beast and took off with it. A badger, normally weighing in at twenty pounds, is pretty hefty cargo, but add a struggling badger to the equation, and the eagle was having one hell of a job dodging badger teeth and claws to remain airborne. The eagle fought to gain altitude for a minute or two, then dropped his contesting load onto the road below. End of the eagle's badger problem. End of the badger's eagle problem.

The golden eagle is a creature of open spaces, both in the skies and in its hunting grounds. Can we learn how to live without "befouling and denuding" our environment and provide for the eagles' continued existence in our land? Will we stand this test of whether or not we are truly civilized?

Preview of a Riparian Forest

I t was cold in Wickenburg when I met up with friends to carpool out to the Harquahala Mountains near Aguila, Arizona. We planned to spend time hiking a canyon, studying plants as we went along. Our leader had never been there before, but others in the group had. She led us by virtue of her knowledge of plants.

Once there, we moved slowly. No need to rush about after the focus of our attention today. Plants are nicer to track than birds or animals. Plants stay put. They give you good looks all the time.

One of the first we learned was the desert trumpet, also known as bladderstem, Indian pipe-weed, or *Eriogonum inflatum*, for the Latin-loving scientists amongst us. It wasn't in bloom. Too early in the year yet. But its bulging stem shooting up from a basal rosette of leaves was easy to identify. Parts of the stem were inflated and hollow, a feature typical of many of the *Eriogonum* family members. Arizona is home to about fifty of their number.

There are wasps that take advantage of these hollow stems. They bore into the cavities and fill them with captured insect larvae and their own eggs. Once they've provided food for the eggs laid, their job is done. The plant houses and protects the rest of the process.

We paused at a place in the canyon where huge boulders had tumbled during a recent rain, gouging out a portion of the drainage. Just above the avalanche, water seeped from a spring, providing enough moisture to sprout one cottonwood and nine willow saplings. Tamarisk had also taken root. Now, tamarisk is an invasive, not a plant native to our area, and several of our group were volunteers from the Hassayampa River Preserve where they periodically indulge in tammy-wacking to remove tamarisk in order to assist the survival of the indigenous willow and cottonwood trees. They felt obliged to remove the tamarisk at the spring to give the native trees a better chance.

No one had a clue how the tiny sprigs had arrived here or survived the past summer. The spring didn't seem large enough to continue to provide in drought conditions. There were certainly no nearby stands of cottonwoods or willows for miles. Yet here they were, starting life under marginal conditions and seemingly out of nowhere.

It remains to be seen whether these upstarts will become the great trees their genes destine them to become. Wouldn't it be grand to visit the Harquahala Wilderness Riparian Forest one day?

Hey. It could happen!

He Just Wore Out

Today I spoke with a woman I used to work for. I call her every February, on her birthday. I haven't seen her in nearly a year. She used to live in Sun City West, a retirement community, with her husband. He had Parkinson's disease. That's why I knew them.

He had difficulty walking and experienced some mental impairment, so she wasn't comfortable leaving him alone when she went out to run errands or play bridge with gal buddies. I was doing companion care work at the time, providing respite for caretakers, and she called me to stay with him when she went out.

When I met him, he was already very disabled, but I enjoyed the time I spent with him. Some days we sat together on the back patio, watching quail scurrying between backyards, me chatting about whatever came to mind, since he was not able to keep up his end of a conversation very well. Other times I read to him from the newspaper or his favorite magazine, *Arizona Highways*. He loved looking at the pictures of places that, sadly, he would never be able to visit anymore. Laboriously forming the words his mind wanted to say, he told me how he planned to take a trip to this or that scenic spot in the near future--and did I want to come too? I always said I'd love to and we'd go just as soon as he was a little stronger.

When I fixed him lunch, it was usually a bowl of soup, which he enjoyed and could still manage to eat. He spooned it carefully, cautiously, into his mouth. Bad days, though, he'd suck it up through a straw, then spoon the vegetable and noodles.

Only one time was he strong enough to go for a short trek using his walker. We traversed the driveway and he toiled down the sidewalk, me keeping pace, past a couple houses before we turned and went back. I marveled aloud at the feeling of warm sun on our skins and picked up some seeds shed by his neighbor's palms to plant in my own yard.

As often as I offered to take him out for a "walk" in his wheelchair, he refused. Pride, I think. If he couldn't go under his own power, he wouldn't go at all.

Lots of times, I just sat with him while he watched TV, never quite sure how much he was comprehending, but there to help if he needed anything or had to go to the bathroom. I threw in occasional comments about whatever we were watching, something requiring no more than "yes" or "no" answers. In that way, we could converse.

When he turned ninety, family came from all over the country to celebrate with him. They took him out to dinner. He was pleased, but exhausted by the evening. He did know everyone, though, which was a delight for all.

Once I found a scrap of paper, fallen to the floor. It was a short note he had scribbled, perhaps only to himself.

Perhaps only to see if he could, indeed, still write. He had painstakingly scrawled how a man, once so high, had been brought so low, so low, so low. I knew he'd been a wealthy, powerful, esteemed Chicago lawyer in his heyday. He obviously still had enough about him to rue his current state.

His wife's daughter lived in central Phoenix and often came to her mother's assistance when she felt overwhelmed. She wanted her mother and step-dad to move closer to her, where she could be more readily available in emergencies. He didn't want to go, but he just didn't quite realize how difficult it was becoming for his wife to take care of him. She didn't want to leave her support system behind either, the friends from Temple, and bridge. Eventually she decided moving was the most sensible thing to do.

An apartment downtown was remodeled for them, to accommodate the wheelchair. They sold the house in Sun City West, and moved out of my life, except for the occasions I phoned to find out how they were doing.

After only a few months, my ex-employer told me she'd found her husband outside with his walker, heading down to the corner, intent on buying a paper. But what corner? What newstand? He didn't have a clue where he was or was going, just hellbent on getting there. She knew then she was in over her head. She had to find a nursing home. With her daughter's help, she found a small center nearby which specialized in care for Alzheimer's and Parkinson's patients. She went to visit him daily, driving herself, though she too was now ninety.

I went to visit him once. I don't think he knew who I was.

He got excellent care, but was never in good spirits, I was told. He refused to participate in activities and stopped talking to anyone. Wheelchair bound, he was up and dressed by staff each day, but ate hardly enough to keep body and soul together.

His wife told me that eventually, he just slept when she visited, never rousing to even open his eyes in acknowledgment of her presence.

A month or two after he died, she called to tell me. "He just wore out," she said.

She had a stroke the day after he died and could not attend the funeral, which was in Chicago. She felt lucky, though, for she had no enduring paralysis and was slowly getting better. Her mind, she told me, seemed to work more slowly. Sometimes she couldn't come up with the word she wanted. She had assistance from aides only during the day now, having dismissed the ones who had been staying the night. She slept well and didn't need their help any more. She still used the walker, but sometimes forgot it as she moved through the apartment. She needed it to make her visits to the man upstairs, though. He'd recently lost his wife and was depressed. She thought it helped, somewhat, when she called on him. She looked forward to having her son visit for a few days around her 91st birthday. That was next week. Her grandson from Israel was coming the week after.

I said I was sorry to hear about her husband. That's the polite thing to say. But I also told her I was glad-- because he was just so "wore out."

Alex Longoria, MSW, a community social worker, has written: "Modern science has brought us great success in the battle against the illnesses that plague mankind. Unfortunately, we have artificially increased longevity, but in the same act we have also multiplied long-suffering. There is the long-suffering of the patient who is not cured, but remains in a state of suspension, neither healing or dying."

I'm just glad my friend's long-suffering is over. I've a little palm tree growing in my front yard to remember him by.

First Snow

Since we were desert rats, I considered this annual trip to be an educational requirement. Each winter my son and I would spend a weekend in Flagstaff, Arizona to play in the snow. Charlie, his friend from pre-school through middle school, accompanied us most years. Now and then we got snowed in and had to miss school on Monday while snowplows scraped exit routes from the high country, an acceptable hazard as far as the boys were concerned, and one I could live with too.

We found a hill south of town that became our traditional spot for tobogganing. Out in the woods, away from residential areas, we had the place to ourselves. It was a real challenge. Dodging trees was imperative and some years, a bit of a thaw put the end of our run into a pond. Sliding too far meant a cold, wet landing. Sledding 101.

My son's edification began the very first trip, the very first experience. The boys were about five at the time. Charlie had seen snow before on a family outing. He regaled Pat with tales of snowmen, snow angels and snowball fights. These whetted Pat's desire for his own first contact. Ever the competitive one, he was sure he could outdo Charlie at any snow sport and ached to prove it.

Our first sighting of snow as we traveled north was spotty patches left in the shade of Ponderosa pine. Shouts of anticipation from both boys begged me to pull the truck over so they could play in it, but I urged patience, to wait until we found thicker, less icy places. They were placated for the moment, but had a tough time sitting still, just watching all that precious snow zip past the windows as we sped up the highway. A few miles later the snow field was solid and they convinced me they would surely die if they couldn't stop to make one quick snowball or two to satisfy their souls before continuing on to "Flag."

I pulled off at the next rest stop. The parking area had been cleared by a snowplow. Snow was piled in hedges along the edges of the lot. Before I had the truck parked, the boys were racing away, taunting each other over which of them would get to the snow first.

Pat won. But having watched one too many cartoon characters dive into snow drifts after penguins, he tried to leap head first into the berm--only to bounce off. He turned to us, a shocked, ego-injured expression in his face and said, "Man, that stuff is hard!"

Charlie and I laughed ourselves sick.

All Kinds of "Firsts"

Awinter trip to Sulphur Valley, south of Willcox, Arizona, netted me lots of "firsts." My main purpose was to witness large flocks of Sandhill Cranes. I'd heard how dramatic they were in their take-offs and landings when in large numbers. So I went.

The playa near Willcox is winter headquarters to many species of birds, but it's a Sandhill Crane extravaganza. Fields of grain are left for cranes to glean, the modern day equivalent of the native grasses that provided fodder for millions of years, and the cranes take full advantage. For two and a half million years this prehistoric study in gray has been visiting the playa. Three feet tall, with a wingspan of seven or eight feet, you'd think they'd be easy to spot in migration, but since they fly at altitudes just below commercial airliners, they are too high to see from the ground until they land. Landing is a process. Lifting off is too.

Flocks number in the thousands here. The birds are most often heard before they are seen as they begin unfolding from the sky, because they seem unable to flap their wings without telling their companions all about it. I listened to their rattling vocalizations all through my lunch without seeing a single one. It wasn't until I visited the fields where they strolled looking for grain that I got to see why. They can't rush.

It seemed impossible any birds could be feeding,their numbers were so great and they were so tightly packed. An ocean of liquid, cosmic mercury in the stubble left of harvested corn, they flowed over the land. As I watched, the edges of the undulating sea began noisily peeling off the field to be folded into the blue of the sky, the volume of their squawking increasing tenfold in their panic. It was like watching a wave form and depart into the ethers in a column that snaked back and forth across the sky in layers, gradually spiraling higher and higher until they were out of sight. My guide said there had to be an eagle abroad, since only a predator would bring about such a response, and sure enough, a bald eagle sailed over us. It made no attempt to hunt, but the cranes weren't taking any chances. Everyone wanted the improved safety of huge numbers in flight, but it was impossible for that to happen all at once. Over the course of an hour, all the cranes departed earth for sky. By that time, those first in flight were descending again. It was incredible.

Another first sighting I had was a Crissal Thrasher. As I skirted the edges of a farm, crunching through winter-dead leaves below a row of cottonwood trees planted as windbreak, scouting for owls reputed to be in the region, a Crissal perched before me. Right out in the open, it "mooned" me, then sped for cover. Its rust-red butt is a diagnostic field mark. I was delighted to make its acquaintance because I'd been missing this bird for ages. On a Christmas Bird Count near Arlington, every other person in the group I was with saw this thrasher and I did not, though I was right there with them. Fate shat on me that day, though I saw every other kind of thrasher, including the Sage. It happens. But I had my day in the Sulphur Valley. A Crissal at last.

I also saw my first White-tailed Kite--living up to its name too. It hovered over the grasses after leaving its perch on a dead branch, acting for all the world like a tethered balloon, kiting on the wind, eying the earth for prey. What a beautiful bird that is. Black shoulder epaulette on gray jacket, over white underparts. Eyes of fire. No mistaking this foot-and-a-half-long missile for anything but a predator.

Then the ravens. Here, in the grasslands of southern Arizona, the Chihuahuan reigns supreme. It resembles the Common Raven I'm familiar with, but is smaller and more communal in habit. It too was a "first" for me.

So many new birds for me in a landscape older than God to wintering cranes. May they share it with us for another 2.5 billion years. At least.

Three Elder Trees

Ancient Fremont Cottonwood trees have thick, deeply-furrowed, gray-brown bark. Their trunks can be four feet in diameter and support a canopy of leaves reaching 100 feet high. The leaves are broad, shiny and triangular in shape, turning a golden hue in the fall before carpeting the ground in winter. In spring, before leaves bud out, flowers form. Trees are male or female. The female is the one that scatters cotton-like seeds to give the trees their name. They need lots of water, so they live in wetlands, along streams and rivers, at altitudes ranging from 150 to 6,000 feet above sea level. They are favorites of beavers for food and dam building. The Hopi Indians use the roots for carving Katchinas, the doll-like representations of their gods.

The Fremont is the variety of cottonwood in residence at the Hassayampa River Preserve south of Wickenburg, Arizona on Hwy. 60. There's a place along the trail to the pond (imaginatively labeled a lake) where a huge Fremont stump tilts toward the path. Its trunk, a good twenty-three inches in diameter, is severed cleanly, no doubt because it was deemed a threat to passersby. There it sits, a mere shade of its former self, never destined to achieve the grandeur of a four-foot trunk or 100-foot height.

But on the north side of the stump, a sucker sprouts.

* * * * *

The Blue Palo Verde is a member of the pea family, but that's only obvious if you happen to see it in bloom, in April or May. The yellow blossoms are five-petaled and shaped like those of sweet peas. It is Arizona's state tree and grows at altitudes of 500 to 4,000 feet. Perfectly adapted to an arid life, it loses its leaves during droughts, helping to retain moisture by cutting down on surface area. Photosynthesis continues unhindered in the green branches and twigs of the hardy tree, each twig defended by a quarter-inch thorn at each node. Fertilized flowers form flat, brown pods of seeds, important food sources for a number of animals including indigenous people.

Seeing an old Blue Palo Verde, gnarled trunk up to a foot and a half in diameter, branches reaching thirty feet high, bursting forth in spring bloom is a glorious sight. A feast for eyes and insects.

Walking a major wash near my home one afternoon I happened upon just such a monster palo verde. It had grown in the steep bank of the wash, the trunk crooking out of the bank's side, then straightening toward the sky. Over long years it became top-heavy and the crooked trunk cracked right at the bend, toppling the bulk of the tree into the sandy wash. The bark was split at the crook in a gash that appeared to run the circumference of the tree, but the trunk's interior fibers still held and pumped life to the limbs. Evidently, this rupture was an old one. There had been little rain for at least a year, but where the branches plowed into the gravel, erosion had scooped sand and rock away. The tree must have been quite an obstruction when water did flow, but so far the branches had not been totally severed from the roots. Until that day, the tree lives.

Upstream a ten-foot tall Mesquite tree has washed down the arroyo, almost to the downed Palo Verde. When the mesquite hits that obstruction, perhaps in the next big runoff, the two trees will make a very effective dam. Their collision may be what finally takes out the palo verde completely. Just briefly, perhaps we'll have a lake forming as water backs up behind the trees, a fitting memorial to a grand and stubborn elder palo verde tree. Until that day, the tree lives.

Springtime Composite

There's a nest under construction in the scrawny palo verde. It's in a tree that literally crawled out from under a rock because it sprouted from below a river boulder I transferred from a nearby drainage to edge the driveway. Add to that the fact that I have to trim it to keep it from growing into the path of vehicles and its enormously deformed appearance is explained. It's uuugggly. Nevertheless, this is the second year cactus wrens have preferred it as a nesting site.

Last year's abode is decayed, but still present. It continues to sport the tinsel its residents considered the height of fashion and so wove into the grasses and weeds forming the walls of their football-sized artificial cave. I feared the "pretty" they so cherished might ensnare their young when they got large enough to fledge. It could get wrapped around a foot or some other body part, so I tried to remove it. No go. It was interwoven so well it just stretched until it hung, fluttering in the breeze, an even worse danger to the babies. No problem. Mom and Dad just reworked it into the mix, and it remained a heady part of the decor. Now, though, it's "so last year," and another homesite is underway. I'm fine with that. I enjoy them as neighbors; it's their taste in trees I question.

There's also the fact that male house sparrows are in constant hot pursuit of any female. All of those (the females) are fleeing at breakneck speed through bushes and trees. The ladies don't look all that willing, but their ardent, persistent suitors don't seem to be leaving them any choice.

The Saye's phoebe pair is hanging around the house again too, though they seem only window shopping for a dwelling place. They call endlessly to one another, "Will this do? How about here?" It's been months since I've seen them about, but that nesting urge must be strong. I hope they've forgotten about last year s site on top of the garage door opener. The garage was such a mess until childrearing was over. I'd like them close by, but not that close again.

The female cardinal has been absent all week. There's the male, collecting seed, bright red except for his black mask and throat. He's leaving and coming back for seed again, so perhaps he's already making meal runs for her as she sits on eggs.

My dog is visiting the Big Galleta again. He buries his face in the upper, dry stalks, searching for the heart of the clump, where green is again sprouting, spring tonic for canine browsers. Proof of more renewed life.

An antelope squirrel creeps cautiously around creosote, casing the area for dogs before stuffing a kernel of old, dry dog food into its bulging cheeks to hide in a secret buried cache, hoarding against seasons of want. It seems early to see them out and about, but winter was mild, and I guess today *is* warm enough. No snakes yet. But active squirrels mean the snakes that eat them are not far behind. Have to start watching where I step.

With very little rain for the last three months, it's doubtful there will be many spring flowers, but a recent shower has coaxed some creosote into opening a few tender, yellow blossoms.

A tiny annual, sporting miniscule white, star-like flowers--always among the first of spring--has trusted fate and made a dash for reproduction. The flowers are so small I need a magnifying glass to get a decent look at them. I wish I knew what they are, but can't find them in any books or the wisdom of any person I know.

The fiddleneck's in bloom, but not the long curving cascades of yellow flowers. Only a single blossom for each stunted plant.

The mallow's small and sparse yet. The only good looking plant is the one just outside the fence around my garden, where I'm surely watering it. Oh well. It may be the one thing I water the squirrels won't eat.

Too early for the cactus to be flowering yet. The hedgehog hasn't begun to form buds at all, and they are always first to blossom. For me, they are the sign of spring's true arrival, that the annual cycle--birth to rebirth--continues.

A loggerhead shrike! Distinctive and regal in his gray/black/white attire. A year- round resident of my desert, but not one I often see around my house. Frequently mistaken for a mockingbird, a second look reveals the black mask, a hooked bill and chunkier build. He sometimes hunts smaller birds, using his strength to bludgeon them to death once caught. Nicknamed "the butcher bird" he often leaves an insect or small prey item hanging on the barbs of fences for future snacks. Usually, the shrikes are silent. Once mates are found and territories established, they are in hunting mode and seldom chat. Now, though, he sings his full repertoire, impressive, but hardly lovely. His odd vocalizations run more along the lines of squeaks and screeches, unappealing to me, but they must please his lady and tell other shrikes what turf's his. He's another sign the season's changing.

A pair of red-tailed hawks is hanging out together. They float in the air, rising, then plummeting in impressive displays of flight. They may be looking over a particular mesquite tree as a nesting site. There's a house being built next door, human in origin. I hope the hawks won't be discouraged and leave.

Yep. Signs of spring are upon us. But I insist its not here until the hedgehog blooms. Just because.

Phoebeville Revisited?

Two days ago I heard a *purrrting* sound in the garage. I stood in the kitchen, a closed door between me and the noisemaker, and since I couldn't immediately recall where I'd heard it before, it seemed wise to keep the door closed. I listened closely. Was it a bird? A snake? A bird hollering at a snake? The garage was open to the desert surrounding my house. It could have been any of a number of critters on the other side of the door. All my speculation, though, was getting me nowhere.

Finally, I carefully opened the door a crack and spooked a Saye's Phoebe from the top of the garage door opener. It continued *purrrting* at the top of its lungs. Was it announcing its intention to remain? To occupy the territory? There was no nest under construction, and I still don't see one, but this morning, as my son left for school, he mentioned he'd spooked a phoebe from a perch on the garage opener days earlier, and that it had been singing like it had something important on its mind.

Dear God. Does it all begin again?

Crazy

I saw a sage thrasher for the first time on the Christmas Bird Count in the Wickenburg area, north of my home by about 45 miles. Then again a week later in the Arlington Christmas Bird Count, near Buckeye. It must be *the* bird of the winter, because I saw another last Sunday. It sat on the top of a dead mesquite in a neighbor's yard. Silent, this winter visitor from northern sage country indulged me in a long, leisurely look. Sand-colored above. White wing-bars. White chest and belly streaked with milk chocolate spots. Definitely a sage thrasher. Three sightings in one month!

Now, I've an abundance of curved-billed thrashers in my neck of the woods, but this was a first sighting for me of the sage. It was perched near a home under construction. An unusual bird near an unusual house, being constructed by an unusual man.

In talking to him recently, this neighbor told me he suspected I was an ex-Roman Catholic nun who got thrown out of the convent. He figured I was insane, a crazy. I've no idea what I did to obtain this evaluation. He didn't specify what had brought him to his conclusions. But, I think he's crazy too. Maybe we're both right

Every conversation with him is unique. He once killed a man, he says, and did time. Incarceration convinced him that coyotes and other wild creatures as neighbors are preferable to humans. Humans just get him into trouble. He's been in Vietnam, he claims. Has five kids, all grown. No wife, currently, but he lives with an older woman. He claims to be sort of a lover/caretaker for her. But he only lives with her when the weather is extremely cold or hot. The more comfortable seasons he's in the "house" he's building on his property to the east of mine. It has no plumbing, no plans, no electricity, no foundation either. Painted bright green, it's a three-storied, ramshackle plywood affair, with a fourth story in the planning so "he can look down on his neighbors" more effectively. He assures me he doesn't need blueprints or permits because he leases his land to a rancher for grazing purposes and this exempts him from having to comply with the same laws as the rest of us. I have no idea of the veracity of any part of his story. Much sounds imagined, but who knows? Maybe he does have five kids.

The fact that he likes collecting large, run-down vehicles is not imagination, though. He has buses, cars, trucks of multiple tonnage, most of which barely run. None would pass emissions tests, but since none are licensed or registered, who's to know? He claims he doesn't have to mess with those rules because he lives in a rural area. It's okay for him to drive in to town to pick up the recycled newspaper from the bins he maintains to make a living. It's everyone else that needs to be registered and bother with emission testing. The irony of his stance is lost on him.

Everything he says comes out many decibels louder than most people talk. And he has a pure brilliance for sticking his foot in his mouth. He stopped by my house once to borrow my phone. Meeting my son for the first time, he blared, "Well, you look like you're used to the good life." I have no clue why he said that. Pat later told me he'd started to get offended, then considered that perhaps the guy simply meant he had all his teeth. If the "good life" meant that, then perhaps the kid's right. Our neighbor certainly does not have all his.

The roads in our homeowners association are privately owned and our Board is currently embroiled in arguments with non-members and realtors of properties to our east who want to use our roads to access their property, for which, it seems, legal access has never been provided. My non-conformist friend, who lives east of us, is our Board President's staunchest supporter regarding the sanctity of our roads. He repairs barbed wire fences cut when landowners drag trailers down our roads to set up homes in areas outside our homeowners association. He drives nails through boards and places them in roads where his immediate neighbors will puncture their tires. It doesn't seem to occur to him that hikers and animals might also be maimed, though I've pointed that out to him. He just doesn't want to see the land east of our development settled. He wants to maintain the limited number of people, the desert views and wild desert inhabitants around him. So it's fine for him to use our roads to access his property because of his status as self-appointed security patrol, but not anyone else.

I can relate to his goal, though not his means. It's one thing my crazy neighbor and I have in common. We'd both like to protect the desert around us from becoming another subdivision, squelching our rural ways and the lives of the plants and animals we've both come to love.

With that much in common, I'm compelled to beg leniency for us both. We assess land values not by amounts tallied by the state treasurer or the size of the transaction at the time of sale. We count land value in wild animals living on it and whether or not it's fit habitat for snowbirds like sage thrashers.

Hey, we *are* both crazy.

In Between

This morning I could sit outside with my morning coffee *sans* coat. That's an indicator of spring.

Yesterday's walk brought me a shrike vocalizing from a hackberry bush. It was so focused on song that I came within 15 feet before it was aware of my presence and fled. As I moved closer to the hackberry, another shrike flushed and flew after the first. So--a pair. Another indication of spring.

My neighbor and I have ventured into wine making. Our first project is elderberry wine. We need temperatures between 68 and 75 degrees to keep the yeast happily procreating in our "must"--the name for the slop in our five gallon jug that's our wine-in-progress. This rules out wine production in the summertime because we both keep our houses at 80 degrees to ward off air conditioning bills that would necessitate a second mortgage, settling instead for bills that merely cause weeping and gnashing of teeth. The warm temperatures of the last week brought our must to dangerous degrees, so we borrowed a tub from another neighbor in which to soak our carboy--the brewing bottle. That's brought down the temperatures enough to keep the yeast happy. But that's another sign of spring: temps too high for wine generation.

On the other hand, the sage thrasher I saw last week is a winter visitor to our area, and he's not yet flown. White-crowned sparrows are still here too, not headed to arctic breeding grounds. White-winged doves aren't back from their Mexican winter headquarters, so spring isn't utterly sprung. My final proof is the hedgehog cactus. Its blossoms mark spring's arrival, in my opinion. Nary a bud on them yet, so they're not convinced.

Not winter, not spring--it's the season of "in between."

Accomplished

Silence descends
Over shrike's oration.

Hours of petitioning
For a mate
Have produced a companion.

No further need to boast.

Again

What joy. Hooray!
That February day
To hear Saye's phoebes trilling away
In trees pleasantly far, I pray,
From my garage. To nest, to stay,
Somewhere else is quite okay.

Hope's undone.
The nest's begun.
Apparent to practically anyone,
Grass deposits about to be spun
Into a nesting phenomenon
Top the door opener, once more overrun.

House Gods

The keeping of sacred nooks for graven images in a home is typical of many cultures. Each house has its own gods, charged with protecting the occupants and the abode in which they are honored. Sometimes the gods are associated with ancestors of the current occupants, but in any case, these gods are fed and tended in order to obtain their blessings and good will.

My neighborhood has house gods too. Ours take the form of Saye's phoebes. They dwell with us whether or not we're wise enough to honor them. They bless us regardless.

I have a pair taking up residence in my garage. I assume it's the same pair that nested there last spring. Their finely woven cup of a home is almost complete.

My neighbors have a pair that's taken a liking to a porch light. They too are returning to last spring's nest site. They too seem willing to cope with human comings and goings in their near vicinity.

On morning walks I pass another home with a pair of birds that *peeeers* at me mournfully until I'm gone. I can't see a nest, but there's got to be one.

Last week I gave a boy a ride home from the bus stop. As I pulled into his driveway, who should be standing watch but another Saye's phoebe. Then I spotted its mate wing-dancing through a nearby bush. Guardian spirits on task.

Today I passed the ribs of a house under construction and saw another pair in attendance. House gods awaiting the completion of their temple.

Ancestors? Maybe.

Relatives? No doubt.

Gods? Utterly.

Mistaken Identity

"I saw a raven yesterday," my friend began. At least I think it was a raven. They're all black and have short tails, don't they?"

"They are all black," I replied, "but they are good-sized and don't have short tails. The starling is black and short-tailed. Might that have been what you saw?"

"It was big and it cawed," she responded.

"That settles it, then. It must have been a raven. That's the only thing around here that caws. I can't explain the short tail, though."

Our conversation continued as we moved slowly down the road. She'd seen me walking the dogs and came out to report on our project. Our batch of elderberry wine is a first for us both and it's housed in her garage. After delivering her report on the fermentation process, her cawing mystery bird was the topic.

I glanced at the low hills to the west of us, a rocky ridge of broken lava. There perched a large, black bird with its profile to us.

"There's a raven," I pointed to our obliging example. See? No shortage of tail."

The raven turned toward us and spoke in a strange chortling. It was new to me and I was surprised by it. It continued for a minute, then hopped into flight and passed directly over our heads, gurgling all the way. Once past us, it reverted to cawing, which it continued until it was out of sight.

"I know where I've heard that before," I realized. "I've heard starlings making that call."

Ravens are imitators. Starlings are imitators too. So who's imitating whom? An edge of uncertainty and a reminder that reality is porous had been introduced into my morning. It was delicious.

Seeing the Light

I reviewed the materials sent me regarding a whole foods supplement a friend was selling and called her to say I'd like to try her product. She was delighted and effusive. "I'm so glad you saw the light!" she declared, then went on to tell me how to take it and discuss the purchase plan by which I'd buy it.

"Saw the light?" I asked. "Do you really equate taking this product with 'seeing the light?' What light?"

"Yes, I do," she answered. "I went to church all my life and never 'got it.' I never understood. I don't want to sound ridiculous, but now I find myself doing special little ceremonies, honoring my food, blessing it with gratitude for the good it will do my body. I find myself wanting to do the best I can for myself and being grateful for everything I have. My health has improved in so many ways, clearing up problems I didn't even know were there 'til they left. I'd be crazy not to take this product for the rest of my life, and I know I will. Through taking it, I finally 'got it' and 'saw the light.'"

I was amazed and amused. Food supplements?

I too was churched as a child and attended organized religious services faithfully for the first half of my life. Now I see myself as a worshipper in a larger, all encompassing church--Nature. That's what informs and reminds me that all is sacred. I 'got it' as a child in church and continue to 'get it' whenever I commune with nature, something that feels more right for my needs at this stage of life. I agree with Ansel Adams, who said, "The clear realities of nature seen with the inner eye of the spirit reveal the ultimate echo of God." Enough said.

But food supplements?

There are any number of paths for "getting it." To some extent, we're all in the process. Perhaps none of us is ever finished the learning, or the making of inner connections that manifest the sacredness of the "Big Picture" to each individual. I know I'm not finished.

But come on. Whole food supplements?

I remember a friend telling me of a conversation she overheard as a child between her father and a Roman Catholic nun. They were discussing the presence of a revival tent in their community. Her dad was questioning its value. The nun said, "After all, my friend, do you really think the Lord cares by which path any one of us comes to Him?"

So why *not* whole food supplements? Truly, the Creator works in mysterious ways.

Spring

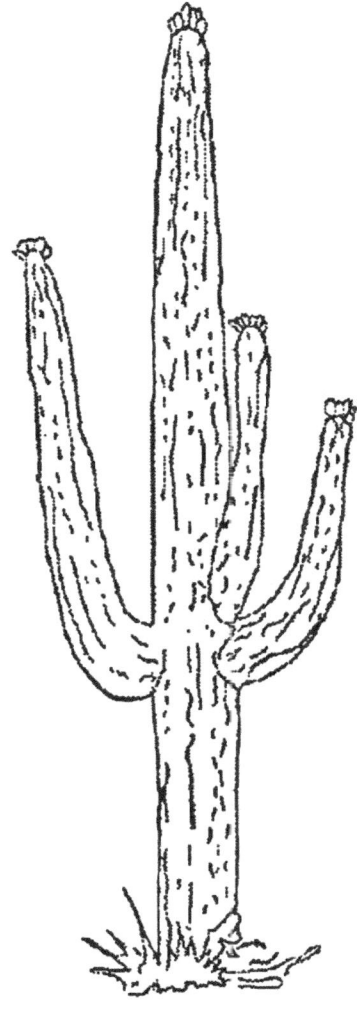

It's Official

St. Patrick's Day dawned cloudy and rainy, a much needed reprieve from the dust. Almost a third of an inch has fallen in the form of a light misting the Navajo call "female rain." It's intermittent and a little too late to assist spring annual production, but the creosote are encouraged to flower. Trees and cactus, which flower later than the annuals, can take advantage too.

The leaves on the ends of branches on the ironwood are yellowing and dropping off. Years ago, when I first witnessed this, I worried the tree was diseased. Now I know this is preliminary to the formation of buds, whose purple splendor will soon coat the final foot of each twig. Give it a month and this legume will be in bloom, playing host to bees and other insects, one of which is a butterfly colored exactly like the blossom it sips. Made for one another.

Cactus wrens have filled the depths of their nest in the palo verde tree with squalling voices, only temporarily silenced when parents stuff a hapless insect down their throats. The young are insatiable.

Curve-billed thrashers are already being followed by offspring as large as they are, as they dart through bushes and scurry along sandy paths. The babes fly almost as well as parents, but still hound incessantly to be fed. Their begging haunts Mom and Dad's every move.

Cattle grazing the open range to the east have a number of small calves with them. The mothers try to keep them hidden behind their own bodies, or in clusters of trees along washes. Craning their necks to see over the creosote, the better to watch my approach, the moms are part curiosity, part consternation at the sight of me with my umbrella. Eventually they decide not to chance my intentions and stampede to what they deem a safer location.

The Saye's phoebe nest in the garage looks finished, but is eggless. Haven't a clue what's holding up the action there.

The pomegranates and crepe myrtle in my yard have budded in new leaf. The roses are bushing with growth and have formed flower buds.

Soon the seeds in the garden will show their faces above ground. Maybe the additions I made to the fencing will ensure I get more of the fruits of my labor this year.

So, this St. Patrick's Day, as I climb the road cresting a saddle in the hills to the south, what should I find? A hedgehog cactus in bloom. Flaunting its royal purple on a number of spine-filled arms. The first I've seen this year. Since this is my arbitrary symbol of Spring's arrival, I declare the season sprung.

Another annual cycle complete. Birth to death, then rebirth.

"As it was in the beginning, is now, and ever shall be. World without end. Amen." . . .

And so the world goes round and round,
(In) every time and season...
And so through every time of life,
To him who acts with reason
The beauty of all things doth appear.

"The Seasons"
Traditional nineteenth century English verse